THE MAGIC THAT CAME TRUE

ANDREA RANKIN

G2 Rights Ltd

THE MAGIC THAT CAME TRUE
Copyright © Andrea Rankin 2014

First edition published in the UK in September 2014
© G2 Rights Limited 2014

Print Edition ISBN: 978-1-78281-123-7

G2 Rights Ltd, 7-8 Whiffens Farm, Clement street, Hextable, Kent BR8 7PQ

THE MAGIC THAT CAME TRUE

ANDREA RANKIN

THE MAGIC THAT CAME

TRUE

Andrea Rankin

This is a story about a girl called Gail and her dog, Dylan. At the time this story begins, they were living in a really bad place. Drug addicts would be outside the close waiting until Gail and Dylan went out. They would shout at Gail, calling her names. Gail would walk on, trying to ignore it, but then they would start to throw stones and even bricks at her.

It got so bad that Gail couldn't go outside during the day. She only went out at night when most of the time it was quiet and she could take Dylan for a really long walk. They would be out for hours, walking at least six miles every night.

During the day Gail would let Dylan out on to the veranda as much as she could. She knew it wasn't fair on him, but life was scary. She thought about giving Dylan to someone else so that he could have a better life, but she couldn't do it. She loved him too much. At the end of the day they had no where else to go.

Gail was quiet and very thin. She had blue eyes and long brown hair and always wore jeans and a blue jacket. Dylan was a stunning dog, an Alsatian-Collie cross. He was a real character, and if Gail gave him a row he would answer her back. She thought it was rather funny.

One night just before midnight, Gail decided it was time for their walk. 'Come on Dylan' she said, and Dylan jumped up in excitement, wagging his tail. She put her headphones on just in case she saw any of the drug addicts. She would wear them when she had to go out during the day as well to try and drown the noise out from them shouting at her, but she could still hear them shouting faintly.

Everything seemed quiet that night. When they came back, as on most nights, it was dawn. Gail gave Dylan some breakfast and then made herself a cup of lemon tea. After she had finished it she fell asleep on the sofa. Dylan came into the living room and lay right beside her. Soon he was asleep too.

When Gail was dreaming she saw herself standing next to an ocean with Dylan beside her. It felt as if they were in a cartoon. When Gail looked at Dylan he was a cartoon character, but when she touched him he felt the same as in real life. She could see her reflection in the water and saw that she was a cartoon character too.

'This is weird', said Gail out loud. But the place was beautiful. The sand was like real gold and it was gleaming from the sun. She bent down to touch it and as she lifted some and put it in her hand she saw that it really was gold. As she looked around she noticed that the trees and the grass and even the flowers were all cartoonish.

She didn't want to wake up from this special dream. She wished so much that she and Dylan could stay there forever, but she knew it was only a dream. She felt much safer and Dylan was so much happier.

Gail saw a cottage in the distance. 'Come on Dylan, let's go and have a look' she said. The cottage was painted yellow and the front door was white. The windows had white curtains on them, but again none of it looked real. It was all cartoonish, like everything else.

As Gail and Dylan went up to the cottage, the door suddenly opened by itself. Gail called out, 'Is anyone there?' There was no answer, so she and Dylan went in, to find that, strangely enough, everything was real. The living room was decorated lilac and had white flowers on the wallpaper. There was a lilac sofa and a white carpet.

Gail went into the kitchen, where the wallpaper was yellow with pale blue flowers on it and all the kitchen units were white. There was a fridge too, and when Gail opened it there was food in it. It was all vegetarian, which seemed a coincidence, because Gail was a vegetarian. In the middle of the kitchen there was a yellow table with yellow chairs and a bowl of fruit on the table. On the worktop there was a white kettle and in the corner of the worktop there was a yellow microwave.

When she opened the cupboards there were cups and plates and lots of dog food for Dylan. 'Dylan, do you want some dinner?' Gail said. He barked. 'I take it that means yes', said Gail, and he barked again.

She noticed a white bowl on the kitchen floor and picked it up to see that Dylan's name was on it in gold writing, so she put some food in the bowl for him and said, 'Here you are Dylan.' Then she put the bowl back on the floor. She opened one of the cupboards to see if she could find some tea and noticed there were a few jars of Lift lemon tea there.

'I don't believe this' she said out loud, 'this is what I drink!' So she made herself a cup of lemon tea and a sandwich. She then opened the back door and went out into the garden. It was a massive garden and in the garden there was a white bench. Gail went and sat on it and Dylan lay down on the grass beside her. The sun was nice and warm.

A while later she and Dylan went back into the cottage. Gail went up the stairs and entered one of the bedrooms. The wallpaper was blue and had dolphins on it. Gail was thrilled, because she loved dolphins. The carpet was a deep blue colour. She sat down on the dolphin cover on the bed, then lay on the bed, and Dylan jumped up and lay beside her.

Half an hour later she got up and went to the bathroom. It was all tiled, even the floor, in pale blue. Gail really liked it. As the sun shone through the bathroom window she could actually feel the heat on her face.

There was a shower in the bathroom, so she took a shower and afterwards opened the glass door and got out. She dried her face and body, and even though it was all cartoonish her skin felt real, even her hair felt real. She opened the bathroom door and Dylan was sitting waiting on her. 'Hi Dylan' she said, going into the bedroom and opening the wardrobe. For some reason she already knew that there were some clothes in it. She got dressed, and then she noticed a blue bandanna on the bed.

'This is strange isn't it Dylan? This wasn't here before' she said. 'I think you should have this.' She put it round his neck and said 'You look so handsome, Dylan.'

'Woof woof!' said Dylan as if to say 'I know I do.'

'Want some dinner Dylan?' said Gail.

Dylan barked, jumped up on Gail and licked her face. They went downstairs and Gail went into the kitchen and made some pasta and vegetarian sausages for the both of them. Gail said, 'Here you are Dylan', and put the food in his bowl. Gail then sat down at the kitchen table and ate hers.

When they had finished their dinner she and Dylan went into the living room and Gail watched the television for quite a while. She couldn't understand why she hadn't woke up yet from this amazing dream. A while later she decided to go to bed; the time was now eleven twenty.

'Come on Dylan, let's go to bed' she said, and they both went upstairs to the bedroom. Gail got changed into her pyjamas and got into bed. She was afraid to go to sleep because she knew that when she did wake up she would be back in reality, with the drug addicts giving her a hard time and no peace at all. She was trying to stay awake, but she was really tired. Dylan lay beside her with his head on her arm and both of them fell asleep.

Morning came, and Gail woke up and let out a big yawn. To her surprise, she was still in her dream. But was it a dream? She rubbed her eyes and then looked again just to make sure that she was in the same place. She was.

She got out of bed and got dressed, and Dylan woke up and jumped off the bed. Gail hugged him and said 'I think this is our new life Dylan, I don't think we need to go back there any more.' Dylan licked her face. 'C'mon, let's get some breakfast.'

They went down the stairs into the kitchen and Gail put the kettle on. She made some toast for herself and a cup of lemon tea, then opened the back door and went outside. It was a lovely, sunny day. She went and sat on the bench. Dylan came out the back door and sat beside her.

A while later Gail decided to take Dylan for a walk. He was very excited. His tail was wagging and he was jumping up and down. They went towards the ocean. It was so blue and clean, and when Gail approached the water she could see the different colours of coral underneath the water. As she started to walk again little birds flew by her, but again they weren't real but like cartoon birds. They also saw rabbits, but they too were cartoonish.

As they walked on a little grey squirrel came up to Gail. She bent down and stroked its head. The squirrel went in front of her and Dylan and kept looking back at them both. Gail kept walking and said 'C'mon Dylan', as she looked to see where the squirrel was. She noticed he was sitting still on this colourful path. As Gail got closer the squirrel moved again, as if it wanted her to follow him.

She now came to some trees, and as she touched one of the trees it felt real, though it didn't look real. It was cartoonish, like everything else.

When she got past the trees she noticed an extraordinary garden. There were so many different flowers, most of them white, and there was a massive dolphin waterfall you would be able to stand under for a wash. It was blue and white. The water that was running from it was so shiny that it didn't look like normal water. There was something different about this water; Gail could sense it.

She went over to it and put her hands under it and it was like glitter falling on her hands, just like little stars. Then all of a sudden her hands became real again.

Gail decided to put Dylan under the waterfall, so she called him over. 'Come over here' she called. She lifted him and said, 'Gosh Dylan you are heavy!' She put him under the dolphin waterfall and when the glittering water went all over him he too became real.

Gail smiled at him and lifted him out of the waterfall and put him down. She said, 'Look at you Dylan, you're real again!' She hugged him and said, 'Let's go back to the cottage.'

They made their way back home. When they finally reached the cottage Gail couldn't believe how her life had changed. Part of her was afraid that at some point she would still wake up in her old world.

It was getting late, so she went back into the cottage and made some dinner. She called to Dylan to come in and get it. He came back into the cottage and went straight to his bowl.

As Gail shut the door she noticed the stars appearing in the sky. Though darkness was setting in the stars were so big and shiny that they lit the whole place up. It was really amazing to look at.

After Gail had watched some television, she decided to go to bed. Dylan followed her up the stairs and into the bedroom. As she got into bed Dylan jumped up and lay beside her, and eventually they both fell asleep.

Gail was dreaming again. She saw herself back in her old life, packing things away. It was as if she was watching herself from the fantasy world, but in her dream she was really there and Dylan was with her.

When she had finished packing she left the flat and went to her mother's house. She knocked on the door and when the door opened her mum, Ellen, was standing there.

'Hi Gail, come on in' she said, so Gail and Dylan went in.

'Mum, I have to talk to you.'

'What is it, Gail?'

'I'm leaving with Dylan and I won't be back to stay ever again.'

'What do you mean Gail?' her mum asked. 'What's going on?'

'Mum, it's too complicated to understand, you'd never believe me.'

'Gail' said her mum, 'Try to explain to me, whatever it is I know that I'll believe you.'

'I can't mum' said Gail. 'I came to say goodbye and that I love you and that you don't have to worry any more Mum, I'll be safe.'

'I will always worry about you Gail and nothing will change that' her mother replied. She knew she had to let Gail go. She hugged her and stroked Dylan's head.

'I need to go now Mum' said Gail, but before she went out of the door she turned around and said, 'Some magic can come true. Look out for me in your dreams and you will see how happy I am. Goodbye mum.'

'Goodbye Gail' said Ellen with tears in her eyes.

Gail woke up, and for a moment she thought she was back in her flat. But as she became more awake she realised that she wasn't, and sighed with relief. She somehow knew that the dream had happened for real and it was as if she had actually been there. She hoped that she would see her mum again, even if it was only in her dreams.

She got out of bed, went down the stairs and put the kettle on. She heard Dylan coming down the stairs, and he came straight into the kitchen.

'Hi Dylan, want some breakfast?'

He barked as if to say yes. She gave him some cornflakes and made toast for herself and a cup of lemon tea. Afterwards she took Dylan for a walk down by the ocean and then headed towards the dolphin waterfall.

As they walked something made Gail turn around. Out of the corner of her eye she noticed a white cottage in the distance, surrounded by forest. Just then she realised that they weren't alone.

She decided to walk towards the cottage. As they got closer she could see how big the front garden was. There were so many different colours of flowers, and it looked outstanding. As she was admiring the cottage she happened to look at one of the windows and noticed something strange. The glass of the window seemed to move like water. Gail approached it and as she put her hand on it her hand suddenly went right through it; she realised it really was water.

She took her hand out of it, thinking to herself how weird this was. She approached the front door and knocked on it. Someone called out 'Come in', so Gail opened the door and was about to go in when she thought to herself that she had better ask if it was OK to let Dylan come in. Just as she was about to ask a lady called out 'Yes you can bring your dog in.' That was spooky, thought Gail.

'I'm in the living room, two doors on your right' said the voice.

Gail went into the living room and there was an old lady sitting on her wooden rocking chair. She was wearing a dark blue plain dress. Gail approached her.

'It's nice to meet you, I'm Gail' she said.

'It's nice to meet you too, I'm Katie. Please sit down.' Gail sat on the sofa. 'So tell me Gail, how do you like your cottage?'

'I love it Katie, and Dylan seems to love it too.'

Katie stroked Dylan and said 'You're a lovely dog, aren't you Dylan?' Dylan licked her hand and wagged his tail. He then sat down right beside Gail and wouldn't move.

'How do you keep him so white?' asked Katie.

'Well he basically keeps himself clean' said Gail.

'His brown ears feel like silk.'

'Yes they do, don't they.'

'I take it you have been in the dolphin waterfall, because your skin is real?'

'Yes I have, and I put Dylan under the waterfall too. I've got to admit it was strange being a cartoon character. When I was younger I loved watching cartoons and used to wonder what it would be like to be in one, and in a way I am in one now.'

'Yes Gail you are, but the difference with this cartoon is that it's special and it can all become real. You see the same thing happened to me when I arrived.'

'Katie, can I ask you something?' said Gail.

'Yes Gail, what is it?'

'Was it you who put the food in my fridge and freezer and the dog food in the cupboard?'

'No Gail it wasn't me.'

'Then who was it?' asked Gail.

'No one, it was already there for you' said Katie.

'I don't understand' said Gail.

'In this world you'll learn that things just appear and also you can wish for anything you want.'

'Are you serious Katie?'

'Of course I am.'

'How long have you been here Katie?'

'Quite a long time now. You see, just like you I came here in a dream. I was going through a very hard time and I was just about to give up, I didn't want to exist any more. My marriage had fallen apart a long time ago and he had become abusive towards me. I tried to leave him but he followed me and it didn't matter where I would go he would always find me.

'Anyway I was sitting in my apartment and I had a big bottle of whisky and a bottle of tablets on a table beside me. I remember being so tired that I fell asleep in the chair. When I woke up the next day I was here, sitting on this rocking chair and believe me, I thought I was still dreaming, but luckily I wasn't and I've been here ever since. I was the first to come here, and now you and Dylan are the second and third. It is only special people that are allowed to come here.

'You see Gail, you have something magical in you like me. It was the magic

11

that brought you here. I watched you struggle Gail, I would see you trying to cope with the drug addicts outside your house and I would see them giving you a hard time. Sometimes I saw you in your dreams. I was there trying to reach you but you never saw me. When I first came here I didn't know what was going on, but inside my cottage there was a big white book that lay on the table in the living room. The writing in front of the book is in gold and it says 'Special Magic' on it. Inside the book it tells you why you were chosen and why I was chosen too.'

Katie got up from the rocking chair and said, 'I'll just be a minute Gail, I'm just going to get the book.' A couple of minutes later she came back into the living room holding a book. She sat down next to Gail on the sofa and opened the book. A shower of glitter fell from it.

'Where did the glitter come from?' said Gail.
'Did you put it in the book yourself?'

'No. You see this is no ordinary glitter, it's magic glitter and part of the book. Watch this Gail.' She put some of the glitter in her hand and blew it away. Then all the glitter was making sounds like musical chimes.

'Wow, this is incredible!' said Gail. 'Look Katie, they are changing colour. They were silver and now they are gold.'

'Yes, I know' said Katie, 'It's really quite spectacular.'

Katie showed Gail her name inside the book when she was born, which was 16.4.1967. It also said that while Gail was being born in reality, her spirit was also being born in her dream world. It said that when Gail came here in her dreams to stay, that back in her old life she was considered to be dead because no one knew where she had gone or where she was. There was no trace of her any more, but in her dream world the spirit of her would grow stronger and she would have powers that would help to change things.

'I can't believe what you've just told me Katie.'

'Well Gail it's all true. I'll show you Dylan's name now.'

She got to the page where Dylan's name was. His date of birth was 5.8.1992, and when Dylan was being born he was being reborn in his dream world too. That had also made Dylan's spirit grow stronger. In Gail's eyes Dylan was a unique dog and in many ways more like a person. His last owner had abused him and then moved away and left him to defend for himself. Dylan became a stray, but soon he was picked up by the RSPCA. Gail at that time had just lost her dog Rex, and the way she was feeling, she wasn't ready for another dog. The place where she was staying was scary and her friend Joyce thought it would be better for Gail to go and get another dog, so Gail ended up going to pick another. As soon as she saw Dylan she went up to him, and strangely enough the look he gave her was the same look Rex had given her, as if it was meant to be. So Gail took him home and even though life was hard for her, at least she could give Dylan a lot of love and a new home that would last forever.

'I think it's amazing that this book knows all about us' said Gail.

'Yes I suppose it is' said Katie. 'Well, I think I will make us some lemon tea, would you like a cup Gail?'

'Yes, that would be nice Katie.'

Gail gave Dylan a big cuddle and said 'Your my special boy, aren't you Dylan?' He licked her face and gave her a paw. She looked into his big brown eyes and said 'How could anyone hurt you Dylan?' She stroked his head.

Katie came through with the tea and some sandwiches on a tray and put it on the table. She then went back into the kitchen and brought through some biscuits for Dylan. When Katie went to close the book a glow of light came from it, so she opened it again. The gold writing in it disappeared and then all of a sudden a woman's face appeared. She looked like an angel.

'Who's that?' asked Gail. Just as Katie was about to answer, the woman in the book began to speak.

'Hello Gail, it's such a pleasure to meet you' she said. 'My name is White Angel and I'm here to watch over you and Katie.'

Gail's face suddenly went pale. 'I know this has been a lot for you to take in, but you have been sent here for a reason' said White Angel. 'Please don't look so worried, you'll be fine. I have to go now but I'll be seeing you very soon.'

The face disappeared suddenly and then the gold writing reappeared. 'Are you OK Gail?' said Katie.

'Yes I'm fine, I'm just a little stunned, that's all. I need a whisky.'

'I'll go and pour you one' said Katie. She came back

with a glass of whisky. Gail thanked her.

'So tell me, who is White Angel, Katie?'

'She is a witch' said Katie.

'A witch?'

'Yes, but she's a good witch.'

'That's a relief.' said Gail. They both smiled at each other.
'Would you like another whisky Gail?' asked Katie.

'No, I think the one I had was enough because I'm
feeling a little light headed, but thanks anyway.'

A while later Katie made the two of them something to eat
and gave Dylan his dinner. After they had eaten they sat and spoke
for a while about their pasts and talked about all the bad things
that had happened to them. Then Gail noticed the time.

'Look at the time Katie, it's eleven forty five' she said. 'I'd better go now.'

'Ok Gail, will I see you tomorrow?'

'Your probably will' said Gail. 'Goodnight.'

'Good night Gail.'

Gail and Dylan made their way back to the cottage. As Gail looked
up at the stars she saw that it was a clear night and the ocean was all
lit up. The sand was glistening like gold. It was such a view.

They finally got home. Gail gave Dylan some biscuits and a drink of
water. She made herself a cup of lemon tea and went upstairs to go to
bed. She got changed into her nightgown and got into bed. She finished
drinking her tea and put the dolphin cup on the table beside the bed. Dylan
jumped up onto the bed and lay beside her. They soon fell asleep.

As Gail was dreaming, she could see her mum in her back garden hanging
out her washing. She kept looking around as if she knew something was there.

'Mum!' called Gail.

'Gail?'

'You can hear me mum!'

'Yes I can, but I can't see you Gail.'

'I'm high up in the clouds Mum, looking down.'

When Ellen looked up she could see Gail's face; her eyes were full of tears. 'Don't cry mum, I'm happy now' said Gail. 'Please believe that.'

'Gail, can you come any closer?'

'Maybe in my next dream. I've got to go now Mum' said Gail. 'But I'll come back and see you soon, I promise.'

Just then Gail woke up and looked at the clock. The time was five forty-five am. She got out of bed and went down the stairs and made herself a cup of lemon tea. She sat down at the kitchen table and did some thinking. She really missed her mum. She wondered if the dream was actually real. To her it seemed very real, as if it was alive. She knew that somehow she could go back to her old life and would be able to see her mum all the time, but knowing that she would have to go back sometimes sent a shiver down her spine. Gail knew she was settled for life now and that she would never leave this magical world.

She heard Dylan coming down the stairs. He came straight through to the kitchen and straight over to Gail and licked her hand.

'Morning Dylan' said Gail, and she stroked his head. Dylan followed Gail everywhere. It was as if he was scared that Gail would leave him because that was what his last owner had done to him. But Gail adored Dylan and would never do that to him.

After breakfast Gail took Dylan out for his morning walk. As usual it was another sunny day. She and Dylan went towards the ocean and when Gail stared into the water looking at the different colours of coral she suddenly felt as though she was being hypnotised. She was so relaxed and tears were running down her face for no reason. Then she started smiling. Gail then moved away from the water and a few minutes later she snapped out of it.

Dylan approached her with his ball and dropped it right in front of her feet. 'I take it you want to play Dylan' said Gail. 'Woof woof' said Dylan. So Gail threw his ball for him. When she finished playing with him she decided to go for a paddle in the water. She took off her sandals and went into the water. She didn't go too far because for some reason Dylan was wary of the water. As Gail went a little further into the ocean it was so clear that she saw something gleaming at the bottom of the ocean. She put her hand down into the water and picked it up. It was an enormous gold key.

'I wonder what this is for Dylan?' said Gail.

'Woof' he said. The gold key looked so new, there wasn't a touch of dirt on it.

Then Gail heard Katie call to her, so she got out of the water. 'C'mon Dylan', she said, 'let's go and see Katie.' So Gail and Dylan went towards the cottage and the door opened. 'Katie, is it OK to come in?' shouted Gail.

'Yes I'm in the living room, take a seat Gail. Hello Dylan, you're a lovely boy aren't you?' said Katie. Dylan put his head on her lap.

'Listen Gail, the gold key that you have in your hand, please put it back in the water' said Katie.

'Why Katie?'

'Well you see this key could change our world. It could unlock our dreams, others would appear and it would be destroyed. We have got to keep the key there.'

'OK Katie' said Gail. 'I'll go and put it back in the ocean, I won't be long.'

Gail and Dylan approached the water. Gail took her sandals off again and went in. Where the key had lain before at the bottom of the ocean, there was still a gleaming light coming from the same spot. So she bent down and put the gold key back in the same place, then got out of the water. She put her sandals back on and went back to Katie's. 'C'mon Dylan, let's go.'

When she got to Katie's the door suddenly opened, Gail and Dylan went in and the door closed by itself. 'Katie, that's it done, I put the key back', said Gail.

'I'm in the kitchen Gail, making some tea.' So Gail went through to the kitchen.

'I'm so sorry Katie for taking the key out of the water' she said.

'It's OK, how were you meant to know? Anyway you've put it back, that's the main thing. Here, I've made us some tea and sandwiches, let's go into the living room.'

'Would you like me to take the tray?' asked Gail.

'No no, I can manage.'

So they went into the living room. Katie put the tray on the table. She gave Dylan a couple of the sandwiches, which he finished in seconds.

'Katie, can I ask you something?'

'Sure, what is it Gail?'

'How do you know about the key?'

'Well Gail, I know because it is written in the white magic book and believe me everything it says is true.'

'I'm just thinking, Katie' said Gail, 'what if the next person that arrives moves it?'

'Don't worry, it will be a while yet before someone else arrives. We will work something out.'

'I like your white sofa and your white carpet, but how do you think you'll be able to keep them clean?' asked Gail.

'If they need cleaning, I'll wish for it.'

'I'm just wondering, Katie.'

'What's that my dear?'

'Well, I know that we live in our dreams now, but what I want to know is, will we eventually die? Sorry for asking such a question, but for some reason I felt as if I had to ask you.'

'That's ok' Katie said. 'The answer is no, we will never die because we are in our dreams and in a way it's like we are still dreaming, but our dreams are actually alive.'

'That's incredible' said Gail.

'Yes it is, and I know that this must be a lot for you to take.'

'Yes it certainly is' replied Gail. 'Listen Katie, I forgot to say something to you. I noticed that your windows aren't made of real glass. When I first came up to your cottage I was admiring it and that's when one of the windows caught my eye. I thought it was glass, but then I thought I could see the glass move and it was like little waves. But when I went up to the window to touch it my hand went right through it and that's when I realised that it was water. I apologise Katie for doing that, I know it was rather rude of me but I was curious.'

'It's OK Gail' said Katie. 'If I were you I would have probably done the same thing. Anyway when I first came here to live, the windows were already made of water and I think that's because in the places in which I stayed I always kept my windows locked. Only now and again I'd open them, I felt safe with them locked, you see. Just like you Gail, I stayed in a lot of bad places and when

I arrived here I knew right away that I wouldn't have to lock my windows or my door. Then when I approached my cottage I noticed a window moving. At first I thought the glass was about to fall out, but when I went up to look at it I knew that it definitely wasn't glass. Like you I touched it and my hand got all wet. That's when I realised my windows were made of water. You look stunned Gail!'

'Yes I suppose I am Katie, I just can't believe how special this place is.'

'Would you and Dylan like to stay for dinner?'

'That would be nice, thanks Katie', replied Gail.

Katie went into the kitchen to make dinner. A while later Gail went into the kitchen to join her.

'Something smells good Katie, what are we having?'

'Macaroni and potatoes' replied Katie.

'That's my favourite' said Gail.

'I know.'

'How could you know that?'

'I just do' Katie replied. 'Have a seat at the table Gail, I'm just about to serve dinner.' So Gail sat down and Katie put the food on the plates.

'That looks delicious' said Gail.

'Well I hope it tastes as good as it looks' said Katie.

When they had finally finished Katie said 'So what's the verdict Gail?'

'Let's just say it's the best macaroni I've ever tasted, you did well.'

'Thank you', said Katie. 'Right, I'll do the dishes since you cooked us a meal' said Gail.

'You don't have to' said Katie.

'I want to show my appreciation.'

'OK, if you must.'

Just then Dylan licked Katie's hand.

'Hi Dylan, would you like some macaroni? Come on then.' Katie put some macaroni and potatoes in a bowl for him and put it in on the kitchen floor. 'Here you are Dylan, enjoy.'

'That's all the dishes washed Katie' said Gail.

'Thank you for doing them Gail, now go and have a seat in the living room and I'll bring us some tea.' Katie brought the tea through and put it on the coffee table. 'Here we are Gail, some lemon tea for you and some herbal tea for me.'

'Thanks Katie, oh and that was nice of you to give Dylan some dinner.

'You're welcome Gail' said Katie.

A while later Gail said 'I think it's time me and Dylan went home Katie, I'm feeling quite tired.'

'Ok Gail, maybe see you tomorrow?'

'Yes Katie, see you tomorrow',

Gail and Dylan left and soon arrived back at the cottage. She gave Dylan a drink and then went straight to bed. Dylan lay beside her and they both went to sleep.

As Gail was dreaming she saw herself outside her mum's house. The door suddenly opened and her mother was standing there.

'Hi Gail, how are you?' she asked.

'I'm fine Mum, how are you?'

'I'm OK but I miss you.'

'How come you opened the door Mum, did you know I was outside?'

'I just had a feeling you were there. Anyway come in and I'll put the kettle on. What would you like to drink?'

'I'll have a coffee Mum' Gail replied.

'So tell me what it's like where you are Gail?'

'It's so peaceful and magical, it's a kind of place that you could only dream of, but luckily for me I was chosen to go there to live.'

'There's your coffee Gail, do you want some cake?'

'No mum, I'm fine. I had a big meal today and I'm still full.'

'It's good you're eating Gail because you never ate a lot when you were here.'

'I know Mum, I'm more relaxed now and not so nervous any more and Katie is always giving me food.'

'Who's Katie?' asked Ellen.

'She's a very special person and friend, you would get on great with her mum.'

'It would have been nice to have met her.'

'Well, you never know.'

'Tell me something Gail, would you ever consider coming back to live here at all?'

'No Mum, there is too much evil and cruelty. I wouldn't want to come back Mum.'

'It's just that the rest of the family wondered where you went to.'

'I know Mum, but they wouldn't believe me, and let's face it Mum, who would? They will just need to believe I left and that I don't want to be found. I'm sorry but that's the only way.'

'I understand Gail, I know how you feel, I can feel it from you.'

'I've got to go now Mum, but I promise I will come back to see you again like I did before.'

'OK Gail.'

They gave each other a cuddle and Ellen stroked Dylan. 'I hope to see both of you very soon.'

'You will mum, goodbye.'

'Bye Gail.'

As Gail and Dylan were leaving the house and were walking along the path, they both suddenly vanished.

Gail woke up and looked at the time. It was seven o'clock in the morning. She got out of bed, trying not to disturb Dylan, and went downstairs to make herself a cup of lemon tea. As she looked outside her kitchen window she could still see the stars glistening. She could hear an owl and as she got closer to the window she could see it in the tree in her back garden. It looked as if the eyes were staring right back at her.

She decided to go back to bed for a while. When she went into the bedroom, Dylan was still sleeping on the bed. Gail got into bed slowly so that she wouldn't disturb him. As soon as her head reached the pillow she fell asleep.

When morning came the sun was shining through her bedroom window. She woke up and felt the warmth of the sun on her face. She looked at her dolphin clock. The time was ten fifty-five am. She decided to get up and said, 'C'mon Dylan, let's go down stairs and get some breakfast.'

She made some toast for herself and the dog and then got ready to take him out. She took him a walk along the golden sand next to the ocean and threw his ball for him a few times. A while later Gail and Dylan went back to the cottage. She hoovered and dusted all the rooms, then opened the back door to let Dylan out. She made herself a cup of lemon tea and went outside to sit on the bench. After she had finished her tea she went to water her white flowers, and while she was pouring water on them a thought went through her mind; that it would have been nice if she could have had a dolphin waterfall in her garden. She was very fond of dolphins.

When she finished watering her flowers she turned around and to her surprise there it was, a blue and white dolphin waterfall. It was really big. Gail just stood looking at it. She was so shocked she didn't know what to think.

Dylan went up to the waterfall and took a drink from it. Then he went over to Gail and licked her hand. Gail snapped out of it and went over to see it.

The water that was coming out of it was so shiny it looked like glitter. It was just like the one she had seen near Katie's cottage. When she was looking at it she could have sworn she saw the dolphins move, but she knew that she must have been imagining it.

She went back into the cottage to pour herself a drink of lemonade and from the kitchen window she kept staring at the waterfall in disbelief.

Later on that day Gail took Dylan for another walk. She wanted to explore more of this magical world. She decided to go another way, where there were lots of trees. As she walked among them she noticed that there were quite a few streams and as she went up to one of them she noticed that the water was all different colours, blue, pink, yellow and purple. She put her hands into the water and with one hand she took some water and put it to her mouth and drank it.

'That is delicious' she said out loud. It tasted like fruit. 'C'mon Dylan, come and get a drink.' The dog went over to Gail and stepped into the stream and took a drink. Afterwards he licked his lips.

'Was that good Dylan?' said Gail.

'Woof woof' said Dylan, and he drank some more.

As she walked on she looked at the other streams. They were all exactly the same. In a way it was like a secret place because it was hidden from the trees. Dylan was having so much fun. He always loved being in the woods.

'Well Dylan, I just hope we will be able to find a way out' said Gail. They kept walking for about an hour and a half, until suddenly Gail noticed a flight of white stairs. She and Dylan walked up them and as they reached the top there was a white door. Gail opened it, not knowing what to expect, and right in front of her was her cottage. She couldn't believe her eyes.

She noticed there were a few more steps, so she and Dylan walked through the doorway, down the steps and on to the path that took them back to the cottage. As they got to the door Gail turned around and saw that the steps and white door had disappeared.

'That was incredible' she said out loud. 'What do you think Dylan?' He barked a couple of times, as if he agreed.

She opened the door and they both went in. She made some dinner for them both, and a while later, after they had eaten, she made a cup of lemon tea and went through to the living room to sit and relax for a while. She felt quite tired. She watched television for a while with Dylan beside her. Eventually she and Dylan dozed off.

Gail saw herself walking along a dark passageway. She couldn't see a thing. She felt someone touch her. 'Who's there?' she said. She heard someone laugh, but it wasn't a joyful laugh, it was more of an evil laugh. She was starting to panic.

'Look, who are you?' she said. 'What do you want?'

Just then there was a glow of orange and red light and someone was standing there. Gail could see his red eyes staring at her. He was getting closer. She could see he was wearing a black hooded cloak. She didn't know what to do.

'Gail' he said.

'How do you know my name?'

'I just do, I know everything about you.'

'Who are you?'

'Who do you think I am, Gail?'

'I don't know' she said.

'Yes you do Gail, you just don't want to say my name. I've come to tell

you that you belong with me in my world and one day soon you will join us.'
'Never, never, do you hear me? I'll never join your world!' shouted Gail.

'If you don't I will destroy you.'

'You can try, but you won't be able to' said Gail. She wasn't sure why
she said that. The words just came out. Then all of a sudden the orange and
red colours that surrounded the man started to fade with him and before
he totally disappeared he said, 'See you very soon Gail' in a deep voice.

When Gail woke up the sweat was pouring from her. She was trying
to catch her breath. Dylan started to lick her face. She stroked Dylan's
head. Then she went to get out of bed and suddenly felt dizzy.

She sat back down. Dylan laid his head on her lap and looked at her
with his sad brown eyes as though he knew she had had a bad dream and
was comforting her. But Gail felt as if the dream had actually happened.

She got out of bed and went into the bathroom to have a shower.
Dylan lay at the bathroom door, waiting for her to come out. When
she was done, she opened the door and saw Dylan lying there.

'C'mon Dylan, let's go and get some breakfast' she said. They went downstairs
and into the kitchen. Gail gave Dylan some cereal and then she made herself
a cup of lemon tea and a slice of toast. She wasn't feeling very hungry. She
opened the back door to let Dylan out. She stood at the door looking at the
dolphin waterfall, listening to the flowing water. It made her feel calm.

A while later she went upstairs and got dressed. She decided to go to Katie's,
so they both left the cottage and walked down towards the ocean. They walked
along the sand, then on to the path that took them to Katie's cottage. When they
got to the front door, Gail went to knock but as usual the door opened by itself.

'Katie, are you there?' called Gail.

'Yes Gail, come in, I'm in the kitchen', replied Katie. 'You're just in time,
I'm making some coffee and I even baked a cake, would you like some?'

'OK Katie, that would be nice.' So Katie poured the coffee and cut the cake
into slices and put everything on a tray. 'Let's go into the back garden, it's such a
nice day', said Katie, They went out to the back garden and sat down on some

chairs. Katie gave Gail her coffee and a slice of cake, even Dylan got a slice.

'So you had a bad dream last night' said Katie. Gail just looked at her and said, 'How could you know that Katie?'

'Because I can see into your dreams. Plus, I know the man you were dreaming about. Is he who I think he is?'

'Yes Gail, he is the devil and he wants to take this world from us.'

'But why?' asked Gail.

'Because it's so special. And I also know that he wants the magic book because that's where the powers come from, but don't worry Gail I'll keep the book safe and I won't let him near it. He would have to fight me for it. The strange thing is that the book will only open for you and me, plus White Angel and Dylan of course. In a way the book is alive, so if he tried to open it, it would automatically lock itself and I know he would never destroy it because he wants the powers so badly. If he ever was to take over our world he would turn a magical place into an evil place, all the beauty would be gone. At night when everyone's asleep he goes into their dreams and takes over their minds.'

'I take it he has not been in your dreams, Katie?' asked Gail.

'I have seen him occasionally. He has already tried to take over my mind but I was too strong for him. You see, I had powers I didn't even know existed. He would talk to me when I was asleep saying that I belonged in his world, trying to persuade me to go with him and saying he would make me look young again, and all I said to him was that I would rather die in my sleep than to go with him. I reckon the strength of my powers kept me alive because I think I would have been dead without them, in fact I know that he would have killed me in my sleep if he was able to, but here I am alive and well.'

'Thank goodness for that!' said Gail. 'Something strange happened in my garden today - I was thinking to myself that it would have been nice to have had a dolphin waterfall and not long after I thought that, one appeared.'

'Well I did tell you about things appearing.'

'I know you did, but I was still shocked by it.'

'I take you like it?'

'Yes I do Katie, it's quite spectacular, I've only ever dreamed of having something like that and now that dream has come true. I did notice something strange about it though.'

'What was that?'

'Well, I could have sworn I saw them move.'

'Yes Gail, you would have, they do move now and again and when they do they become real' replied Katie.

'But won't they die if they are not in the water?'

'No, and that's because these dolphins are very different, they have a special skin that keeps them wet at all times. When you see them looking like ordinary dolphins again, go up to them and touch them. You'll notice that their skin still feels very real and wet.'

'Will they eventually die?'

'No Gail, just like us they'll live forever.'

Back home, Gail made some dinner for herself and Dylan. He just loved her vegetarian food. After they ate she and Dylan went into the living room to watch some television. Gail decided to try to use some of her powers, so she closed her eyes and wished for a bottle of white wine. When she opened her eyes, there it was on the table. 'I don't believe it' she said. 'It worked!'

She went into the kitchen to get a corkscrew to open the bottle and a glass. She didn't normally drink much, but that night she ended up drinking the whole bottle and fell asleep on the sofa. Dylan went upstairs and into the bedroom, went over to the bed and with his teeth he got a hold of the quilt and dragged it out of the bedroom, down the stairs and into the living room. With one end of the quilt he put it over Gail's shoulders and with the other end he covered her feet. Then he got up on the sofa and lay beside her.

As Gail was dreaming she saw herself swimming in the ocean. Suddenly the water turned black and a massive shape came out of the water. A cold shiver went down Gail's spine. She was afraid to look, but felt she had to for some reason. When she turned her head to look, there in front of her was a black shadowy figure. She couldn't see the face.

'Who are you?' she said. In a deep, evil voice it replied, 'I want you to come with me now Gail. You know you belong with us, don't you?'

'I remember you from my dream the other night' said
Gail. 'You're him aren't you? You're the devil.'

'Yes Gail, I like the fact you remembered. Now why
don't you just give in? I know the temptation is there. Let's
go to my world, you are after all, one of our kind.'

Everything started to turn black, but just as she was about to take
his hand she heard Katie call out to her 'No Gail don't do it! You
belong with us, not him, think of Dylan, he means the world to you!'
Her eyes cleared again. She put her hand back down and said 'I don't
think so Lucifer, you are not going to have me, do you hear me?'

'Oh but I will Gail. If Katie hadn't called out to you, you would have taken my
hand. If you don't come with me, I will find a way to destroy your precious world.'

He moved closer to Gail and grabbed her throat. 'I sense
your fear and it's strong, be afraid, be very afraid!' Then he
let her go and went straight back into the water.

Gail woke up, the sweat pouring from her. She felt sick and weak and
was also scared and nervous. In a way she felt as if she was back in her
old life again, but she knew she had to be strong and was determined to
help save this perfect new world she had entered. Even if she couldn't
help save it she would rather die than go to the devil's world.

She noticed that her dolphin quilt was over her and wondered
how it had got there. Dylan was at the bottom of the sofa with his
head on top of her feet. She tried to move her feet slowly, trying not to
disturb him, but he woke up. She got up from the sofa and went into
the kitchen to get some aspirin. She had a splitting headache.

'Oh Dylan, I shouldn't have drunk that bottle of wine.' She made herself
a cup of lemon tea as usual and gave Dylan his breakfast. She opened the
back door and noticed the sun gleaming on the waterfall, which made it
look beautiful. The water ran from it all the time, which was quite soothing
for her. She went out the back and sat on the bench and drank her tea.

Dylan came out into the garden and sat beside her. She was so tired that she fell asleep again and as she was dreaming she noticed that everything had become transparent, all the land and the ocean, even her cottage and the sky too. It was so strange. Gail felt inside that it meant something but she didn't know what. She wished she could know these things and understand what was going on.

Everything was like waves, the way things moved just like ripples in the water. She looked up at the sky and she could see a lady with long wavy, fair hair and a long white dress coming down from the sky. Her eyes were so bright that light shone from them. Gail couldn't even see the colour of them. Her feet landed right in front of Gail.

'Hello Gail, I'm White Angel, do you remember seeing my face in the white book?'

'Yes I do remember, Katie showed me', replied Gail.

'That's right Gail. Well I came to meet you in person.'

'It's such a pleasure to meet you, I thought you would've had a broomstick since you're a witch.'

'No Gail that's old fashioned, witches are more modern now. Though I do know a couple of old witches who still use broomsticks.'

'I see' said Gail.

'Anyway, the reason I came to see you is that I want to make your powers stronger.'

'Why?' Gail asked.

'Well in case I can't get to you in time, I've seen the dreams you've had and I know how scared you felt inside. The power I give you will take your fear away, you will feel stronger and able to stand up to the devil. Now take my hands and close your eyes.'

As Gail took her hands White Angel said 'Now hold on tight.' The next thing both of them started shaking and then sparks were flying all around them. It lasted for about twenty minutes. Then the sparks began to disappear and the shaking began to stop.

When it was over White Angel said, 'Gail, open your eyes.' Gail opened her eyes. 'How do you feel?' asked White Angel.

'I feel great, I've got a warm sensation all over my body.'

'Do you remember shaking at all?'

'No, I don't remember that. Is that a good thing?'

'Yes it is, it means you were naturally hypnotised. Remember last night when you were dreaming, you saw that everything was see-through? Well I know you want to know what that meant.'

'Yes I do' replied Gail.

'It meant that our world could turn out like this if Lucifer takes over. Another thing Gail, always check that the golden key is in the ocean, it's important that it stays there.'

'I know, Katie told me.'

'You see' continued White Angel, 'there is a place under the ocean, hidden away, where the key goes into. If it was to be turned we would die and everything I told you would happen.'

'You probably know that I took the key out of the water, but I did put it back right away' said Gail.

'It's OK Gail, I know you did. You weren't to know, you had basically just arrived here. What I am worried about is that the devil may try to reach the key through you by using your mind. You see he can't just come into our world like us, he has to go into our dreams to do that, but if he ever reached the key through our dreams and went to touch it, his hands would evaporate and that's because the key itself has some power. Anyway, I'd better go now, I'll see you soon.'

'OK White Angel, see you soon' replied Gail.

When Gail woke up she was still sitting on the bench in her garden and Dylan was still sitting beside her. 'Oh Dylan' she said, 'I feel as if I've been sleeping for hours.' She got up from the bench and went into the cottage. She went upstairs to the bathroom to have a shower. Dylan as usual followed her into the bathroom and lay at the door. After Gail finished her shower she went into the bedroom and got dressed, then took Dylan for a walk.

They went towards the ocean again. Gail took her sandals off and went in for a paddle. Dylan joined her. She threw his ball for him a few times, and even though they were just paddling they got absolutely soaked.

Gail heard Katie calling to her, so she and Dylan went to see if everything was OK. As they reached the cottage the door was already open.

'Katie, are you there?' shouted Gail. There was no answer. 'Maybe she's out the back, let's go and see Dylan' she said. So Gail opened the back door and there was Katie hanging out her washing. Gail felt relieved that she was OK.

'Hi Katie' she said. Katie turned around. 'Oh hello Gail, how are you?' Katie asked.

'I'm fine, did you just call on me a few minutes ago?'

'Yes Gail, but I used my mind to call on you, I wanted to see if it would work and it has, which is good Gail, because now we can use our minds to talk to each other. It is very important that we can do this because if something bad ever happens and we can't get to each other, we will still be able to communicate.'

'I understand, Katie' said Gail.

'Would you like a cup of tea or coffee?'

'Coffee would be nice. C'mon Dylan, come and get some dinner.'

So Dylan went through to the kitchen and Katie brought the coffee into the living room.

'Would you like a biscuit, Gail?', asked Katie.

'Yes, thanks' replied Gail.

'I heard you spoke to White Angel while you were dreaming.'

'That's right, I did and it was some conversation.'

'Had she come to see you?'

'No, she spoke to me through my mind and told me she had given you more powers, and I'm glad because you will need those powers, especially in your dreams. You know, don't you Gail, that the devil will try to get you to join them?'

'Yes Katie I know he will, but I'm not going anywhere, I belong here, this is my home now.'

'I'm so glad to here you say that' said Katie. 'I promise you that if you are ever in trouble while you dream or even when you are awake, I'll try my best to reach you.'

'Thanks Katie, I do appreciate what you've just said. Dylan and I had better go now.'

'Ok, see you later.'

'Bye Katie.'

So Gail and Dylan went back to the cottage. She opened all the windows and the back door to let some fresh air in, then she went outside to water the flowers and while she was doing that she noticed the dolphins move again. She put the hose down and went over to them. Their eyes looked so sad, as if they were unhappy. Gail decided to try and set them free. She closed her eyes and made a wish for them to be free. When she opened her eyes both of the dolphins started to move about and eventually they removed themselves from the waterfall. They were floating around in the air and went towards Gail. She stroked them and smiled. Their eyes seemed so much brighter and as Gail walked they followed behind her.

She went to front of the cottage and made her way down to the ocean and the dolphins were still behind her. Dylan walked beside her. As they got to the ocean Gail used her mind to lower the dolphins into the water and then stopped her powers. She watched them swimming around in the water, they seemed so much happier now because they knew they were free.

Gail gave the dolphins names. She called them Precious and Lightning. She thought to herself that it was a joy to see them coming out of the water and going so high towards the sky, then going right back into the water again. She knew they belonged there. After watching them for a while she and Dylan decided to go home.

They made their way to the back door, Gail remembered she had left it open, and she and Dylan went in.

Gail looked at the clock in the kitchen; the time was six pm, so she made herself something to eat and gave Dylan his dinner. When she had finished her dinner she went to wash the dishes, and as she looked out of the window she noticed there were two more dolphins on the waterfall. She went outside to have a look and when she approached she saw that they weren't real, or she would have freed them too.

She went back inside, made herself a cup of hot chocolate and went into her living room and put some soft music on, then she sat on the sofa and relaxed for a while. When she had finished drinking her hot chocolate she put the cup on the pine table, put her feet on the sofa and lay down. Soon she was sleeping. Dylan lay on his own chair and went to sleep too. As Gail was dreaming she saw herself walking into her mother's house. Gail entered the living room. Her mother was sitting on her chair looking very down. She went over to her mum.

'Are you OK? It's me, Gail.'

'Hi Gail, I was miles away', Ellen replied.

'I could see that Mum, are you feeling OK?'

'Yes, I'm just tired', Ellen said. But Gail had a feeling it was more than that.

'Mum, do you want me to make you a cup of tea?' she asked.

'OK Gail, that would be nice.' So Gail went into the kitchen and made some tea for them both. She brought the tea into the living room.

'Here you are Mum, drink this up. Have you had anything to eat?'

'Yes, I had something not that long ago.'

Gail knew she had to try and help her mum feel better. 'Listen Mum, I was wondering if you would like to come and see my world and where I live now' she said.

'I would like that very much Gail, you know I've often thought about it, hoping you would come and show me where you live.'

After they had finished their tea Gail said 'Let's go Mum, I can assure you you will love it.' So they went outside the house and stood there. Suddenly a glow of light came out of the sky, beamed them up and took them back to the cottage. Gail, Dylan and Ellen walked out of the light. Then the light vanished.

'Who does the cottage belong to?' asked Ellen.

'It belongs to me and Dylan, this is our home now Mum.'

'Oh Gail, that is a lovely cottage. The view is so beautiful here, everything is so colourful, isn't it?'

'Yes it is Mum, it is definitely a special place. Come inside the cottage and I'll make you a nice fresh cup of tea.'

They went inside and Gail said, 'Why don't you have a look around while I make the tea mum.'

'Ok Gail.'

Ten minutes later Ellen came down the stairs and went into the living room. 'Gail! she called out, 'where are you?'

'I'm through here in the kitchen Mum' Gail replied. 'Well, what do you think?'

'I think all the rooms are really nice and bright, your kitchen is lovely too.'

'Have a seat Mum and drink your tea.'

'You must be so happy here Gail' Ellen said.

'Yes Mum I am happy and so is Dylan, it's the best thing that could have happened to us.'

'You know something Gail, this cup of tea is delicious, it's so fresh.'

'I know Mum, that's because everything is so different here, the water is so pure and clean.'

'Tell me something Gail, does anyone else live here?'

'Yes, there is a lady called Katie, she is such a nice person, she lives in a cottage not far from here. Would you like to meet her?'

Ellen, Gail and Dylan went to Katie's cottage and Gail knocked on the door, which just opened. Gail's mum looked at her.

'It's OK Mum, this happens, don't worry' said Gail. 'Katie, it's me, Gail', shouted Gail.

'Come in, I'm in the living room' called Katie. So they went in and Ellen closed the front door behind her.

'How are you Katie?' asked Gail.

'I'm fine Gail', replied Katie. 'This must be your mum.'

'Yes it is, this is Ellen' said Gail.

'It's nice to meet you Ellen', said Katie.

'And you too, Katie', said Ellen.

'Are you glad you came to see this place?' asked Katie.

'Oh yes, it's absolutely beautiful, it's such a treat to be here, it's a dream come true.'

They smiled at each other. Dylan went over to Katie and gave her a paw.

'What is it Dylan?' asked Katie. 'Do you want a biscuit?'

'Woof woof' barked Dylan.

'C'mon Dylan, let's go into the kitchen and I'll give you some biscuits.'

'She seems so nice Gail, does she look out for you?' asked Ellen.

'Yes she does and I look out for her too' said Gail. 'I still can't believe that I'm in this dream with you, it's so very special, you're lucky that you and Dylan were chosen' said Ellen.

'I know Mum', replied Gail.

Katie returned to the living room with some lemonade. 'I hope the two of you don't mind lemonade, I thought it would be better because it is rather hot today' she said.

'Of course we don't mind' said Gail. 'It's nice and refreshing.'

'So Ellen, you must miss Gail now that you don't see her as often?' asked Katie.

'Yes I do Katie, but I know she and Dylan deserve this life after what they went through back in my world' said Ellen.

'I'm so grateful that Gail got the chance to leave' continued Ellen. 'Thankfully there is some magic in the world and I'm sitting in it. When I go back home tonight at least I will know that such a magical place exists and it will give me hope.'

'What about your family Ellen, have they asked you where Gail is?' enquired Katie.

'Yes they have asked me.'

'What did you say to them?' asked Katie.

'I just told them that she wouldn't be back ever again and that she didn't want anyone to know where she was. I knew they wouldn't believe me if I had told them the truth, they just know that she is safe and that's all that matters' said Ellen.

'Would you ever consider living here?' Katie asked Ellen.

'Yes I would definitely consider it' replied Ellen.

'And if you were to live here it would be just perfect because it would make our world stronger, but don't worry I'm not trying to put pressure on you' said Katie.

'It's OK Katie, I know you wouldn't try to pressure me' said Ellen. 'I tell you what Katie, I'll seriously think about coming to live here, maybe I belong here too, just like you and Gail' said Ellen.

'Mum, that would be great and you would feel at home here' said Gail.

'Let's all go for a walk' said Katie. So they went down to the ocean and Ellen decided to go in for a paddle. Dylan joined her.

'So Katie, what do you think of my mum?' Gail asked Katie.

'She is a very nice lady and I know for some reason that deep down she is unhappy and she deserves to be happy just like us and I also know she would really love it here' said Katie.

'I agree' said Gail. 'But we will have to give her time to think about it.'

'Of course' said Katie, 'and I have a good feeling that she will come to live here. Just think, she would be closer to you Gail rather than you visiting her sometimes.'

'We will just have to wait and see what Mum decides to do' said Gail. 'Anyway, let's go and join her in the water.'

Dylan was loving all the attention from all of them, and water was being splashed everywhere. Eventually they came out of the water absolutely soaked. Katie invited them back to her cottage and offered Ellen a change of clothes.

'I don't think I will have anything that will fit you Gail' she said.

'Don't worry about me Katie, I'll wish for some clothes' said Gail. She closed her eyes and concentrated really hard. When she opened her eyes she saw a pair of jeans and a T-shirt on the chair.

'Gail, you've done it!' said Katie. 'Your wish came true.'

Ellen just looked at Gail and said 'You actually wished for those clothes?'

'Yes. You see I've got powers, and so has Katie. We can wish for anything we want and it appears. And it will be the same for you if you decide to live here. You too could make your wishes come true.'

'That's incredible' said Ellen. Katie went into the kitchen and made some tea. She gave both of them their tea and a slice of chocolate cake. Dylan also got chocolate cake as well. When they had finished their tea, Katie went to see if Ellen's clothes were dry.

'Ellen, that's all your clothes dried' she said.

'That's great Katie, I'll go and get changed in the bathroom.'

'Gail, your clothes are dried as well.'

'Thanks Katie!' Ellen came back down the stairs. 'I'd better go now, but it was a pleasure to meet you Katie. I hope to see you soon.'

Gail took Ellen down to the ocean and gave her a big hug, and Dylan licked Ellen's hand.

'Mum, do you want me to take you back or will you be OK by yourself?'

'I feel brave enough to go back on my own Gail.'

'OK Mum, see you soon.'

Then a beam of light came down from the sky and took her back home. She stepped out of the light and it vanished. She then went into her house feeling much happier, and went straight to bed.

When Ellen woke up the next morning she lay there for a while just thinking, her eyes full of tears. She was so stunned at what she had seen and knew that it wasn't just a dream. Everything she saw was real. She looked at the time; six o'clock, so she got up and went down the stairs to make herself a cup of tea and some toast and sat down at the kitchen table looking out at the back garden. She had done so much work to it. She then went into the living room and put on the television and sat for a while.

Back in Gail's world, it was dinner time and Gail was out in her back garden, picking her potatoes and carrots. She could have wished for them, but she wasn't lazy, and she had always wanted to grow her own vegetables and now she could.

Dylan went over to Gail and dropped his ball at her feet. 'I take it you want to play, Dylan?' He barked a reply. 'OK then' said Gail, so she stopped what she was doing and stood up and kicked the ball for him. She played with him for a good while, and afterwards she picked up her basin full of potatoes and vegetables and went into the cottage to make the dinner. For some reason she felt really hungry. Finally when dinner was ready, Gail put quite a lot of it in Dylan's bowl and then she sat down at the kitchen table to eat her dinner.

When she was done she took him for a walk. They went towards the ocean looking for Lightning and Precious, The dolphins must have known they were there because all of a sudden they jumped right out of the water.

'That was amazing,' Gail thought to herself. The two dolphins came closer to them, so Gail went into the water and stroked them.

'It's so good to see you both in this big ocean' said Gail. They were making beautiful sounds, as if they were communicating with her. Gail then got out of the water and went back to the cottage and changed into her bathing suit, and then she and Dylan made their way back to the ocean. Gail went back into the water, but this time she went further in and swam next to the dolphins. Dylan lay on the sand right next to the water. For some reason he didn't like going too far into the water. He just lay there waiting patiently for Gail. A while later, Gail finally got out of the water and went over to Dylan and stroked him. 'You're a good boy, aren't you Dylan?' said Gail. He barked. 'Well Dylan, that was a treat for me, I've always wanted to swim next to dolphins, and now I have.'

She and Dylan went back to the cottage, Gail had a shower, and then got changed into a white top and a white pair of jeans and took Dylan out for another walk. As they went towards the forest trees, Gail noticed that some of the trees had some white on them. It looked like snow but she knew it couldn't be, because it was hot and sunny. However, it was nice to look at. They kept walking, Gail wondering what else they would see. As they approached the end of the woods, Gail saw something gleaming through the trees. It was a massive waterfall. They both went towards it. Gail saw something gleaming at the top. She decided to go and have a look, so she told Dylan to stay where he was because she didn't want anything to happen to him. As she reached the top, she saw a big piece of rock made of real gold.

'Wow!' said Gail. As she looked down at the waterfall, some of the gold was running through it, making it shinier.

'That's incredible' Gail thought to herself. She went to the edge of the waterfall and bent down to touch the water, and when she took her hand out of the water it was covered in gold. 'I can't believe this.' she said out loud. 'A golden waterfall!'

She put the gold back into the water where it belonged, and then she went back down to the bottom to get Dylan. He was tired, so she decided to take him home.

"Come on, Dylan. Let's go" said Gail
On their way home as Gail was admiring the view she saw white doves flying in the clear blue sky. The strange thing was that she had never seen them before. Anyway, they reached the cottage and when they went in, Gail made Dylan some dinner and herself a cup of lemon tea and some toast, then went into the living room to watch some television. There was a documentary about seals, which was very interesting, however there were some parts that were very cruel, with people hurting them. They were killing the seals by clubbing them to death and taking their fur and selling it to people who would wear it. Gail couldn't understand how anyone could hurt the seals and thinking to herself and knowing

they are such beautiful animals and also wondering how these people could do such an evil thing. Gail's eyes were full of tears. She suddenly had a thought, and said "I know what we can do Dylan. We could save a lot of seals and other animals and bring them here". Dylan licked Gail's face and gave her a paw as if he agreed with her. Gail decided she would do something the next day. She looked at the time, it was ten o'clock at night. She felt tired and decided to go to bed and Dylan followed her. As soon as Gail lay her head on the pillow she fell asleep. Dylan lay beside her and he went to sleep with his head on her shoulder.

Morning soon came and Gail woke up. She looked to see what time it was on the blue dolphin clock and it was nine twenty. Gail got out of bed and Dylan then woke up. They both went downstairs. Gail made some toast for her and Dylan and then made herself a cup of lemon tea and took it into the living room and sat on the sofa. When she finished drinking her tea Gail decided to go to Katie's for a talk.

'Come on Dylan. Let's go and see katie' So they left the cottage and made their way there. As they approached the door, Gail was just about to knock when she could hear Katie telling her to come in. Gail and Dylan went in.

'I'm in the kitchen' Katie called out. So Gail went into the kitchen. 'Hi Katie is that you baking?' said Gail.

'I'm making a cake' said Katie.

'I can't wait to have a slice,' said Gail.

'Dylan do you want a biscuit?' said Katie. He barked as if he was saying OK, so Katie gave him some biscuits and a drink of water.

'Katie, there is something I want to ask you' said Gail.

'What is it?' said Katie.

'Well, it's about little seals and other animals. I watched a documentary last night and it was disturbing what these people were doing to the seals and the baby ones too. I was just wondering if I would be able to save them and give them a better life.'

'Yes Gail, that's a great idea. We can use our minds to save them. Now let's close our eyes and go to sleep and our dreams will take us there.' So they both sat on the sofa and went to sleep, and as they were dreaming they were in Siberia, and it was all covered in snow. As they turned around they could see

37

the adult seals moving about and the baby seals going in and out of the water.

'Now listen Gail, we can go to other places as well, so I think we should go separately. That way we will be able to save more animals. All you have to do is close your eyes and make your wish and when you open your eyes you will be there.'

'What do we do to bring the animals back home with us?' asked Gail.

'All you need to do is make your wish that you want the animals to come back home with you, and believe me it will work. The animals will fall asleep, then they will magically vanish and when they wake up, they'll be in our world.'

So before Katie and Gail left, they closed their eyes and made their wish for the seals, and when they opened their eyes the seals were gone. Gail looked at Katie and smiled.

'I told you it would work didn't I' said Katie.

'Yes you did' said Gail.

'Right Gail, I am going now to save more animals.'

'That's what I'm just about to do' said Gail. 'See you soon Katie.'

'I'll meet you back at my cottage, OK?' said Katie.

'See you there' said Gail. And they both disappeared.

A few hours later Katie and Gail appeared back at the cottage. Katie opened the door with her mind and they both walked in. As they walked into the living room they could see themselves sitting on the sofa, and they were still sleeping. They went over to where they were sitting and like a couple of ghosts, they went back into their bodies. A few minutes later they both opened their eyes, and Dylan was licking Gail's hand.

'Hi Dylan, who's a lovely boy' said Gail and gave him a cuddle. 'Well Katie, did you save a lot of animals?'

'I did, what about you?'

'I saved a lot of animals too, and I'm so glad I did it' said Gail. 'Shall I go and make some coffee?'

'Yes, that would be great' said Katie. So Gail went into the kitchen and made some coffee and then brought it through into the living room.

'I think I should check to see if the animals are OK by using my mind' said Gail.

'That's a good idea,' said Katie. So Gail closed her eyes and concentrated very hard. Her mind was like a TV screen, because when she was checking to see if the elephants were OK, her mind would move on to the other animals. When she was done, she opened her eyes and gave a sigh of relief.

'Well Gail, are the animals OK?'

'Yes Katie, they've all got their own piece of land to move around in and they have plenty of food to eat. I'm just thinking Gail, do you think that some of the animals might turn on us?'

'No, they won't harm us because I put a harmless spell on them for now, until we get something sorted. The way they are now and everything that they went through, I don't think that they would have the strength to hurt us. I know that sounds silly, but looking at these animals I could see how tired they were and how much they must have suffered' said Gail.

'It's such a shame' said Katie. 'You wonder how anyone could hurt any living animal. Most of it is for money or using them for sport, I'll never understand it.'

'Me neither' said Katie. It was getting late, so Gail decided to go home.

'Right Katie, I'm going home to get some sleep, I feel quite tired.'

'OK Gail, will I see you and Dylan tomorrow?'

'Of course you will Katie, goodnight.'

'Goodnight Gail' said Katie.

When Dylan and Gail arrived back at the cottage, she gave Dylan some dinner and made herself some toast and a cup of lemon tea. Afterwards she went upstairs to bed and Dylan followed her. When she got into bed, she picked up her book and read for a while; it was all about ghosts. She was really interested in ghosts and the spirit world. A while later, she dozed off and the book fell to the floor.

The next morning, Gail woke up with the sun shining on her face. She got out of bed and went down the stairs, Dylan following behind her, and went into the kitchen and made some breakfast for herself and her dog. When they had finished their breakfast, Gail took Dylan for a walk and decided to go and check on the animals. As she went towards one of the bears she noticed that the bear was sleeping, so she went up to him and stroked his arm. She had always wanted to touch a real bear. She went to check on the elephants, to find that some of them were walking about and sleeping and the baby ones were playing in the water. Gail smiled as she watched them.

She then went to see how the seals were doing. Most of them were in the water with other seals and the baby seals lying around on the beach. It was nice and cool for them. Katie made sure of that when the seals got there. Once she had seen that the seals were doing fine, she went to check on the other animals. She walked on until she could see the tigers and their cubs. They also were doing fine. She was so pleased that now they were safe and that no one could ever hurt them again.

'They now live in paradise' she thought to herself. Suddenly she could hear White Angel calling to her through her mind.

'Gail' said the angel, 'I would like to say well done to you and Katie for saving the animals.' 'Thank you White Angel, I knew I had to do something to help them' said Gail.

'I can understand that, so I want to make the land even bigger, and you will have more space to bring other animals here. You used your heart to change things Gail, and I think that deserves an extra spell. You will become more powerful, like me. From what I have seen you have the ability to do things right, and also to change things. Now Gail I want you to close your eyes tight and go deep into your thoughts.'

The white angel then appeared right in front of Gail. She took her hands and held them tight, and the next thing, sparks were flying off them both and they were all different colours. It lasted for about twenty minutes. When it was all over the white angel said 'how do you feel Gail?'

'I feel so good, as if a warm glow had passed through my body.'

'Well now you have that special magic in you, it will help you to do more and more tremendous things.'

'Thank you so much white angel, it means a lot to me.'

'I know it does Gail, and it's a pleasure to be able to do this for you. I had better go now Gail, but always remember, I am never far away in case you ever need me.'

Suddenly her feet lifted from the ground and she was high in the air. She flew up into the pale blue sky and went straight through it. Gail and Dylan made their way back to the cottage, and as they were walking by the ocean Gail was looking for the dolphins. All of a sudden the two dolphins came right out of the water. The way they moved was magnificent. She then noticed two baby ones.

'Look Dylan' said Gail, 'Lightning and Precious have had babies.'

Dylan barked a couple of times as if to say, yes I know. Gail decided to give the baby dolphins names. She called the male Blue and the female Pepper. Gail was so happy that Lightning and Precious had had babies, and she felt glad knowing that no one could ever hurt them.

'Come on Dylan, let's leave the dolphins in peace.' They went back to the cottage for more tea and something to eat. She made her lemon tea and sat at the kitchen table looking out of the window.

When Dylan had finished eating, he went over to Gail and sat right beside her and licked her hand. Gail smiled at him and gave him a cuddle and a kiss. Then she went into the living room and put some music on. She had just realised that it had been quite a while since she had listened to music. The soft ballads seemed to relax her.

Gail then decided to do some cleaning. She was just about to finish it when there was a knock on the door. It was Katie.

'Hi Katie, come in. I'll just put the kettle on and make us a cup of tea,' said Gail.

'That would be nice' said Katie. So Gail made the tea and they both sat down at the kitchen table.

'I thought I should come and visit you for a change' said Katie. I hope you don't mind.'

'Of course I don't mind Katie, I'm glad you came to see me. I just realised that this is the first time you've been in my cottage.'

'I know, it's lovely.'

Dylan went up to Katie and licked her hand, Katie stroked him.

'I had a dream last night, that someone else is going to come and live here' said Katie.

'Did you see who it was?'

'No, I only saw the person from a distance' said Katie.

'At least we know it will be someone we can trust' said Gail.

'How long do you think it will be before this happens?'

'Three to four weeks. I'm just wondering…'

'What's that, Gail?'

'Maybe it's my mum.'

'Have you seen her lately?'

'No, I thought I'd give her some space to think about things, but I will make a point of visiting her very soon.'

'It would be nice if it was just the three of us, wouldn't it' said Katie.

'Yes it would be great, but we know it doesn't work that way unfortunately' said Gail.

'Would you like to come to my cottage for some dinner? And Dylan too of course.'

'That would be nice Katie.'

They left the cottage and walked slowly towards the ocean. Katie noticed the dolphins and said 'look Gail, there's the dolphins. Did you take them back with you from one of the countries?'

'No, the dolphins are from the waterfall outside in my back garden. I couldn't handle them being on there, knowing they were alive.'

'That was such a special thing to do Gail. Did you get the dolphins replaced?' asked Katie.

'I did, except this time they aren't real.'

At the cottage, and Katie sent Gail into the living room while she cooked the dinner. About half an hour later she called Gail into the kitchen for a meal of pasta and potatoes, putting some of the food in a bowl for Dylan.

'Isn't it great that we can wish for things now, and that we don't have to go to the shops any more' said Gail.

'Yes it is' said Katie.

'I was so nervous going to the shops, it was such a horrible feeling. Thanks to this world I don't have to live with that feeling any more, and I have noticed that Dylan is so calm now. Before we came here to stay, he was such a nervous dog.'

'Talking about dogs, I was thinking about taking one of the

dogs that we saved and giving him or her a home' said Katie.

'That's a great idea. Do you want to go and see the dogs tomorrow?'

'Yes I would love to' said Katie.

'I've decided to do something special for the dogs. I'm going to wish for a massive house for them and the cats, so they can live in comfort, and I'll wish for the houses to be close by so we can keep an eye on them. At least we know by using our minds we can make them well again and if there is any bruising we can make it disappear. Does it sound like a good idea?'

'I think the dogs and the cats will be so happy, they'll love it. They'll probably think they have landed in paradise' said Katie. Gail just looked at her and smiled.

When they had finished their dinner and washed the dishes they went into the living room and Katie opened a bottle of white wine. 'Here you are Gail, this will make you sleep tonight' she said.

'Thank you Katie' said Gail. They sat and spoke about their pasts for a while, the bad things they had gone through and the funny things they had done. Then it was getting late and Gail decided that she would go and check on the animals.

'Gail, why don't you leave it till tomorrow, then both of us can go and check on them. You look tired. You and Dylan should go home and get some sleep.'

'OK Katie, that's what I'll do, see you tomorrow.'

'OK Gail, see you in the morning,' said Katie. Gail and Dylan went back to the cottage and she gave him a drink of water and a few biscuits, then she went to bed, Dylan following behind her.

The next morning when Gail woke up she had a splitting headache from drinking the wine. 'Oh Dylan I feel terrible, I'll never drink again' she groaned. She went for a shower and then got dressed and went down the stairs to the kitchen to make a cup of lemon tea for herself, then she took some Aspirin for her headache. She opened the back door to let Dylan out and then sat at the kitchen table, hoping that she would be feeling better soon. Dylan came back inside and Gail gave him some cereal for his breakfast. She then looked to see what the time was; eleven o'clock. So she and Dylan left to go to Katie's. Gail was starting to feel a lot better.

They finally reached the cottage and Gail knocked on the door. As usual the door opened by itself. 'Come in Gail, I'm in the living room' called Katie, so they went through.

'Hi Katie, how are you feeling?'

'I'm OK Gail, are you all right you look a little pale.'

'I'm all right, I had a headache but it's gone now thankfully. The wine obviously didn't agree with me,' said Gail.

'I'm sorry for giving you the wine Gail, I just thought that it would make you sleep well.'

'Don't apologize Katie, it's my own fault for drinking it' said Gail.

'I'll make us a coffee Gail, and afterwards we will go and see how the animals are doing,' said Katie. When they finished drinking their coffee they left the cottage and made their way to the animals. As they approached the dogs Gail went closer to one of them, saying 'hello' and stroking the dog very gently.

'It's OK, don't be afraid.' The little black and white collie licked her face.

'Look at his coat Katie, it's so shiny.'

'Yes I can see that' said Katie. Gail checked the dog all over and said, 'Well it seems to be doing fine. He's still a little nervous, but in time that should go away.'

Gail checked on all the other dogs and noticed that they were all doing better. She then closed her eyes and wished for two massive houses for the dogs and the cats. When she reopened her eyes, there in front of her was a big white house and as she looked in the distance she could see the other house near where the cats were. She opened the door and called to all the dogs, and they all went into the house. They all had their own chairs to sit on and all the rooms in the house were decorated. There was food in the kitchen for the dogs. The dogs were so excited that they were jumping up on Gail and Katie.

A while later, when the dogs had calmed down, Gail, Katie and Dylan left and made their way to see the cats. When they got there they noticed a couple of the cats coming out of the catflap. They went straight over to Gail and Katie and were purring at them. Katie bent down and stroked them. They then went into the house and saw that it was decorated too, and that there was food in the kitchen for them as well. The cats had plenty of room to move about, and they all had their own little beds.

'Do you know something Gail, you've done a great job, even

44

though you used your mind to do all of this' said Katie.

'Thanks Katie, said Gail. One of the kittens had a sore eye, so Gail rubbed ointment on it. She somehow knew that the kitten's eye would be better the next day.

'It's such a shame Katie, all these animals just wanted some love and attention,' said Gail.

'Well at least they'll be loved here for the rest of their lives,' said Katie. They went and checked on the other animals and afterwards they went back to Katie's cottage. Katie made some lemon tea and they sat down at the kitchen table and chatted for a while. Dylan was so tired he lay on the kitchen floor.

Back home, later, Gail gave Dylan some dinner and a drink of water, then she went to bed and fell asleep straight away. When Dylan finished his dinner he went up the stairs and into the bedroom, jumped onto the bed and lay next to Gail and went to sleep. As Gail was dreaming she could see herself standing at her mother's house. She knocked on the door and it opened to reveal her mum standing there.

'Come in Gail, it's so good to see you' she said. 'This might sound strange, but I had a feeling you were going to come and see me tonight.'

'I don't find it strange at all, I had a feeling that you knew I was going to come and visit you' said Gail. 'In a way, we were communicating with our minds.'

'That's amazing, isn't it?' said Ellen.

'I suppose it is. Have you made a decision yet about coming to live in our world?'

'Well I do want to, but what do I say to the family about where I am going?'

'Just say you're going to live with me and Dylan and that you want to make a new start for yourself. You will never be ill again mum, and believe me you will be happy. Well. I'd go now, do you want to come back with me?'

'No Gail, give me a couple of days, so that I can say goodbye to the family and my friends.' Ellen's eyes were full of tears.

'Are you sure you want to come with me Mum?'

'Yes I do Gail, and I know deep down in my heart that it's the best thing for me.'

'Yes mum it is, and it's about time you thought for yourself.

Katie will be so happy when I tell her. Anyway I really need
to go now mum. See you in a couple of days.'

'OK Gail, bye.' Ellen watched as a beam of light took
Gail towards the sky, and then it just vanished.

The beam of light reappeared right outside Gail's cottage. She stepped
out of the light and went inside. She then went upstairs and returned
to her body, and rested for a little while. Dylan was still sleeping.

The following morning Gail took Dylan for his walk as usual. As they were
walking by the ocean, Gail suddenly noticed that more and more things were
starting to become real. It wasn't like a cartoon any more, it was as if something
was making the world stronger. The seals were doing fine. Most of them were in
the water and they seemed to be loving it. Gail and Dylan left them in peace.

They walked further on and eventually got nearer to the bears, and watched
them through the trees. They were wondering about, and a few of them were in
the water cooling down. The little bears were playing with each other. As she and
Dylan walked further on again, they saw the elephants and the baby elephants too
walking around on the grass, while most of the other elephants were rolling around
in the muddy water. Gail and Dylan walked for about a mile before reaching
the tigers, which were lying down on the grass. Some of the baby tigers were
trying to play with the adults, but the big cats couldn't be bothered. Gail new that
White Angel would make the land bigger, so that she and Katie could save more
animals. It was such a good feeling for Gail to be able to do this for the animals.

She decided to walk up to the waterfall. When she got there, she took
her T-shirt and jeans off; underneath she was wearing her bathing suit. Then
she went under the waterfall with Dylan. Gail was watching the gold as it ran
through the clear water. There were pieces of gold all over their bodies.

They stayed under the waterfall for quite a while. When they were done
they lay beside it on the grass soaking up the sun. Gail knew that if the sun
got too warm, she had the power to turn the heat down by using her mind.

On the way home they went to check on the dogs. Gail realised that
Katie must have forgotten that she was supposed to have picked a dog
and taken it home with her yesterday. She thought about choosing a

dog for Katie, but decided that Katie should choose her own dog.

They went to see how the little kitten with the sore eye was doing. When they got to the house some of the cats were lying in the garden sleeping, and a couple of them walked over to her. She lifted them both up and went straight into the kitchen. She put both cats down on the floor and then gave all the cats something to eat. She saw the little ginger kitten who had the sore eye coming towards her; his eye was a lot better. She gave him a cuddle and a kiss, then put him down.

When they arrived back at the cottage, Gail gave Dylan his dinner and then she made some macaroni for herself, before going through to the living room, switching on the television and watching a couple of films. The second film was really sad and Gail started crying, so Dylan went up to her and licked her. She gave him a cuddle. 'You always look after me Dylan' she said.

When the film was done, Gail decided to tidy up one of the rooms for her mum, in case she wanted to stay with Gail for a while, even though her cottage would be there waiting for her. She might feel a little nervous at first, but Gail knew that it wouldn't take long for her mum to settle in, especially in a magical world like this. When she had finished tidying the room, she made a mug of hot chocolate and went upstairs to go to bed and read.

An hour went by and Gail couldn't keep her eyes open any more, so she put her book on the table beside her bed and went to sleep. When she started dreaming, she saw herself and Dylan standing in a place where snow was falling everywhere. 'I wonder where we are Dylan?' Gail said out loud. She and Dylan started to walk, and then the White Angel approached her and said 'Hi Gail.'

'Hello White Angel, this is so beautiful, and it's real,' said Gail.

'Yes that's right Gail, it is real,' said White Angel.

'Dylan just loves the snow, he always loves to play in it.'

'I know he does.'

'It was strange to see you walking towards me, because you usually fly wherever you go' said Gail.

'I suppose it is a little strange. Well Gail, how do you feel about your mother coming to stay?'

'I'm so happy, at least now she will be closer to me,' said Gail.

'I know that she is a nice lady, and caring too,' said White Angel. 'I think she's perfect for this world.'

'Do you live here?'

'Sometimes I do Gail, there are so many places for me to choose from that I basically move around a lot, but I must say this is my favourite place. I just love to look out of my window and watch the snow fall down.'

'Is your house nearby?'

'Yes, look straight ahead.' Gail looked and saw a white castle on top of the mountain.

'That is so magical, I feel like I'm in a fairytale' said Gail. 'But I know this fairytale is real. There are so many people who will never know about this world. Can I ask you something, White Angel?'

'Of course.'

'Is there another dream world? But an evil one, opposite to this world?'

'Yes there is Gail, but our world is so much purer and full of beauty. It's bigger too, and in some ways, our world is stronger. In the other world, the people have been bad. Demons go into their dreams and take them back to the evil world. As you know Gail, they want to take our world, but as I've said before we won't let them. For the powers we all have, we can work together and prevent anything happening. Anyway I've got to go now Gail, but listen, if you and Dylan ever want to stay here some time, you're more than welcome.'

'That would be fantastic!' said Gail.

'Dylan would love it too, because it's always snowing here,' said White Angel. 'If you want to come and stay, just call to me by using your mind.'

'I will definitely do that' said Gail.

'See you soon Gail.'

'OK, goodbye White Angel.'

Dylan and Gail played in the snow for a while, and she ended up as white as Dylan. Just then she woke up. 'That was incredible!' she said out loud. As she went to stroke Dylan, he woke up too. Gail looked to see what the time was. It was nine fifteen in the morning. She got out of bed and went down the stairs, Dylan walking behind. She opened the back door and let Dylan out, then she made herself a cup of lemon tea, went into the living room, put the TV on and sat down for a while.

Dylan eventually came into the living room looking for her. 'Hi Dylan, come on, let's go into the kitchen and I'll give you your breakfast.'

'Woof, woof' said Dylan. She gave him some cornflakes and made herself some toast and another cup of tea. She went out into the back garden and sat on her white bench, Dylan lying beside her. As usual it was bright and sunny, and quite warm. Gail was looking at her dolphin waterfall, and she could see the water gleaming from the sun. Dylan went and got his ball and put it down next to her feet.

'I take it you want to play Dylan' she said. He barked, so Gail threw the ball for him a few times.

A while later, they set off to see Katie. As Dylan went and took a drink, two of the baby dolphins appeared out of the water.

'Oh look Dylan, there is Blue and Pepper' she said. Then she saw Lightning and Precious behind the baby dolphins. Gail went into the water with her sandals on and bent down and softly stroked them. Lightning kissed her and Gail felt so touched inside. The dolphins went back deep into the ocean, leaving Gail and Dylan to go on to Katie's.

As Gail walked up the path towards the cottage, she noticed that there were no dolphins in Katie's waterfall. She knocked on the door and it opened as usual, so Gail and Dylan walked in.

'Katie it's me, Gail' she said.

'Come through Gail, I'm in the kitchen. Would you like some coffee?'

'That would be nice,' said Gail. So Katie made the coffee and offered her some biscuits.

'Thanks Katie' said Gail. Dylan went up to Katie and licked her hand and looked at her as if to ask where his biscuits were.

'Do you think I would leave you out Dylan?' he barked a couple of times, as if to say, 'I hope not'.

'I wouldn't do that to you Dylan,' said Katie, so she went into the cupboard and got him some biscuits for him. Then she sat down at the kitchen table.

'I noticed that the dolphins weren't on your waterfall.' said Gail.

'Well Gail, I have done what you did, and set them free. I knew it was the right thing to do because they are real, so by using my mind I removed them from the waterfall. I watched as they were floating beside me, and when I got to the ocean I lowered them into it.'

Gail smiled and said 'Good on you Katie, they'll be so much happier. When did you set them free?'

'A couple of hours ago,' said Katie.

'That's strange, because I've only seen Precious and Lightning and the baby dolphins in the water. I'm sure the others will be there somewhere. I know what I can do, I'll wish to see them in my mind.'

She closed her eyes, concentrated very hard and put her hand across her face. Suddenly she could see the other two dolphins, further ahead than the other dolphins. 'Thank goodness they are all right,' she thought to herself. And then she opened her eyes and said 'It's OK Katie, the dolphins are fine and happy.'

'I'm so pleased and relieved that they are OK,' said Katie. 'Gail, when is your mum coming to stay?'

'It's tomorrow.'

'You must be excited'

'Yes I am, and I know her life will improve and it will be a lot better for her.'

'Do you think she will miss her old life?' asked Katie.

'I know she will miss the family, even her house and the garden, because she did do a lot to it. But she knows deep down that coming to live in our world is the best thing for her.'

'At least we know now who the third person is. In a way I feel relieved that it's your mum Gail, because she is close to you and me and White Angel can trust her' said Katie.

'I'm sure my mum would be glad to hear you say that,' said Gail.

'Have you been to check on the animals?'

'Yes I have. That reminds me Katie, you forgot to choose a dog the other day.'

'I know, I don't know why but it went right out of my head. Don't worry, I definitely still want one.'

'That's good to know' said Gail.

They decided to go to the golden waterfall, as she called it.
So as they approached it Gail said 'Isn't that magnificent?'

'Yes it is. It's also magical, and we are standing here looking at it. We are so lucky,' said Katie.

'Have you already been here before?'

'No, I never really thought about going under it.'

'You don't know what you're missing. Put your hands under it.'

Katie put her hands into the water and said 'Look Gail, my hands are all gold. Look at it glistening!'

'I know, it's quite spectacular isn't it?'

'You're not wrong there Gail, this it's really something special. I think we should have a picnic here, what do you think?'

'I think that's a great idea.'

Katie closed her eyes and wished for a blanket for them to sit on and some food. When she opened her eyes, she saw a blanket on the grass next to the waterfall. All of a sudden a white basket appeared, and in it there was some food and fruit and a flask of tea. Katie and Gail watched as it landed on the blanket. Then they walked over and sat down. Katie noticed that there were plates and another cup at the bottom of the basket. She put some of the cheese sandwiches on a plate, and the biscuits on another plate. Then she poured out the tea. 'Lemon tea Gail, your favourite' she said.

Gail gave Dylan some sandwiches, then she drank her tea. They sat for a good while watching and listening to the sound of the waterfall running.

When it was time to go Katie picked up the blanket and put it in the basket and off they went. When they reached the dogs' house, Katie decided to go and choose a dog for herself. As they went into the house, the dogs were so excited to see Gail and Katie that they were jumping all over them.

Gail went into the kitchen to see if there was enough food for them, and Katie was trying to give all the dogs some attention, but there was so many of them. She noticed from the corner of her eye a little black Labrador pup, who was behind all the other dogs, and was trying so hard to get to her. Katie's heart melted when she saw him.

Gail called out to the dogs to come and get their dinner, so
they all went through to the kitchen, apart from the little pup, who
ran over to Katie. She picked him up and said 'Aren't you just
beautiful! You're coming home with me.' He licked her face.

Gail and Dylan went through to the living room,
and Gail saw the little pup in Katie's arms.

'Katie, he is absolutely gorgeous!' said Gail.

'Isn't he!' said Katie. 'I'm going to call him Blacky.'

'I reckon that's a perfect name for him.'

Back at Katie's cottage, Gail made some coffee for them
both and then gave Dylan and Blacky a drink of water.

'Well Gail, you must be getting excited, tomorrow will
soon be here and so will your mum' said Katie.

'Yes I am excited, I can't wait to see her' said Gail.

'Are you going to collect her or is she going to come by herself?'

'No no I will go and collect her, I wouldn't want her to come on
her own because while she is dreaming, there is a chance that the
other world, the evil world, might try and take her,' said Gail.

'I quite agree.'

'I hope she will like her new cottage,' said Gail.

'I'm sure she will love it.'

'At least her cottage is close to mine, in a way
it might make her feel more at home.'

'Anyway it's getting late, we'd better go ok Gail. Maybe I'll see you tomorrow.'

'I'll bring my mum over to see you, if that's all right,' said Gail.

'Of course it's all right, I can't wait to see her' said Katie.

So Dylan and Gail made their way home. As Gail looked
up at the sky, she noticed that there were a lot more stars
than usual and they seemed to be so much brighter.

Early the next morning she and Dylan were standing outside the
cottage when suddenly a beam of light came from the sky and took them
both. Seconds later, the light reappeared outside her mother's house. Gail

and Dylan stepped out of the beam of light and as they approached the cottage the door suddenly opened and Ellen was standing there.

'Are you ready to go mum?'

'Yes Gail.' Ellen went to lift her suitcase and a couple of other things.

'Mum, you don't need to take anything with you, you will have everything you need there.'

'I know Gail, I just wanted to take a couple of things with me, a sort of remembrance. You understand, don't you?'

'Of course I do Mum.' Ellen locked her front door one last time, and as she was leaving, she turned around and looked at the house, her eyes full of tears. Then she turned.

'Right Gail, let's go to our new home' she said. As she spoke a beam of light came down from the sky and took them back to the dream world. A few seconds later the light appeared outside Gail's cottage.

'Here we are mum, welcome to your new life' said Gail, giving her mum a big hug. 'Wait till you see your new cottage mum. Come on, I'll take you to see it now.'

As they started walking the beam of light vanished. When they reached the cottage, Gail said 'Well Mum, what do you think?'

'This is fantastic Gail, my own little cottage, or should I say big cottage?'

Gail smiled and said 'Let's go inside.' So they went in. Ellen said 'I can't believe it, its all been decorated for me, and furnished as well.'

'Do you like it Mum?' asked Gail.

'I love it!'

'Come on, I'll make you a nice cup of tea in your new kitchen' said Gail. They went through to the kitchen and Gail made a pot of tea.

'Would you like to go outside and sit in the garden Mum?'

'Yes, that would be nice Gail' said Ellen. So they went out into the garden. 'I can't believe how big this garden is,' said Ellen.

'Look Mum, you've got red roses, your favourite.'

A while later they went back inside the cottage and went through into the living room. Ellen sat on the white sofa and Gail took one of the chairs.

'I like the yellow wallpaper, it makes the room nice and bright' said Gail.

'I'm just wondering how I am going to keep the sofa clean.'

'It's OK Mum you can wish for it to be clean.'

'Do you mean I've got powers?'

'Yes Mum, you always had something special, now you will be able to use it. You have always been a little psychic too, and that will become stronger. I'm going to do something, watch this Mum.'

Gail concentrated and put her hand out towards the sofa. As she began to move her hand, glitter fell from it. When she had finished putting the glitter all over the sofa, she did the same thing to the chairs.

'That was amazing Gail, where did the glitter come from?' asked Ellen.

'I just used my special powers' said Gail. 'If you ever spill anything over the sofa or the chairs at least you know it won't stain. In this world you have no worries. You will feel at peace and you will feel young in your heart and your mind. And from now on you won't be tired any more.'

'That's a relief Gail, there is nothing worse than being tired all the time.'

'Come on Mum, let me show you your bedroom.'

As they went into the room, Ellen looked as if she was in shock.

'Mum, are you feeling OK?'

'I'm fine Gail, I just can't believe how nice my bedroom is.'

The wallpaper was lilac, and the bed was made of pine, which had a lilac bedspread over it. There was a wardrobe and a long mirror, also made of pine. The bedroom carpet was also lilac. The strange thing was, Ellen had always wanted a bedroom like that since she had been a young girl, but her parents couldn't afford it because there were so many kids they had to look after. As Ellen grew up, she had her own kids, so she never had any money for herself.

Ellen sat on the bed and tears ran down her face.

'Mum what's wrong, why are you crying?'

'I'm crying with happiness Gail. You see, I've always dreamed of having a room like this, and now I'm actually sitting in it.'

'Well Mum you deserve it.' Gail gave her a cuddle.

'I would just like to say Gail, thank you for all of this,' said Ellen.

'It's not me you should be thanking Mum.'

'Who do I say thank you to then?'

'White Angel, she's the one that made all of this possible. I reckon the best way for us to say thanks is by being good people and also by protecting what we have here, because there is no other dream like it.'

'I can believe that' said Ellen.

'Soon you will meet White Angel mum, and I know she is looking forward to meeting you,' said Gail.

'Who is she?'

'She's a witch, and she has magical powers.'

'A witch!'

'It's OK Mum, she's a good witch. Even though at times she may be far away she still looks after us through her mind,' said Gail.

'That's good to know.'

'There is so much to show you Mum. Tomorrow I'll show you around the place.'

Gail then showed her mum her new bathroom. It had pale green wallpaper with white flowers on it, and there was a shower and a bath too.

'I still can't believe I'm here Gail, it's like a miracle.'

'I know what you mean Mum, I felt the same way as you when I first came here. It will take a few days for it to sink in, but when it does you will realise that this is going to be your new home forever. 'Come on, let's go and visit Katie.'

On their way to Katie's, Gail took her mother by the ocean so that she could see the dolphins. 'Aren't they just magnificent, Mum?'

'They definitely are Gail.'

As they went towards Katie's cottage, something caught Ellen's eye. 'There is something gleaming on top of one of the hills up there.' she said.

'Yes I know Mum, it's a massive waterfall. I'll take you up to see it sometime.'

'I would like that,' said Ellen.

As usual, Katie's door opened by itself. Ellen looked at Gail in astonishment.

'Things like that happen here Mum' said Gail. 'You'll probably notice some other strange things too. Anyway, let's go inside.'

They found Katie in the living room and she and

Ellen greeted each other, Dylan joining in too.

'So Ellen, are you happy that you came here?' asked Katie.

'Yes I am, and I'm excited too, and I don't feel at all tired' said Ellen. 'That definitely makes a change for me.'

'Yes I can relate to that' said Katie, and they smiled at each other. Ellen and Katie were about the same age, but one thing was for sure, they didn't feel their age any more.

'So Ellen, how do you like you new home?'

'I love it Katie, it's absolutely beautiful. I'm just wondering, who builds these cottages?'

'No one,' said Katie. 'White Angel just wishes for them and they appear. You see, we can wish for anything that we want, but Katie and I don't take our wishes for granted, because we feel it wouldn't be right. Did you tell your family that you were leaving?'

'Yes I did, and they were all full of tears. I told them I loved them very much and I also said that at least Gail wouldn't be alone any more. They knew I wanted to go, so they let me, even though it was hard for all of us.'

'You'll still be able to watch your family by using your mind,' said Katie.

'What do you mean, watch them?'

'Very soon White Angel will be giving you some powers, and when that happens you will understand what I meant. It's going to be great Ellen, we will all have a good time. 'Now I'm going to go and make us all a cup of tea.'

'Is there any chance that I could have lemon tea Katie, rather than ordinary tea?'

'Of course you can Gail, I've got plenty of lemon tea in the kitchen cupboard.'

So Gail went into the kitchen to help Katie, and she made the sandwiches while Katie made the tea. Gail then called out to Dylan and Blacky to get their dinner.

'You know something Gail?' said Katie.

'What's that?'

'Dylan is so like a person, because any time I've heard you give him a row, which is not that often, he answers you back by growling at you. He always seems to get the last word in.'

'Yes I know' said Gail.

'I definitely think he has been here before in another life, and maybe he was a person then because he is such an intelligent animal, and he is so protective over you.'

'Yes I know. When Dylan and I stayed in the old world and certain people would stop to talk to me he would be all over me, like he was jealous. It may sound silly Katie, but that's the way it was. I've got to be honest, it made me feel special, because he didn't seem interested in any other human being. The only other person he liked was my mum.'

'Maybe we can find out if Dylan was a person in a past life' said Katie.

'That's a great idea,' said Gail. They took the tea and sandwiches through to the living room. 'Sorry for being so long Ellen, Gail and I got chatting.'

'That's OK Katie, I don't mind' said Ellen.

'We were talking about Dylan. Katie thinks that maybe he was a person in a past life' said Gail.

'That sounds interesting' said Ellen.

'Anyway, Katie thinks we should try and find out.'

'I agree, this sounds really fascinating' said Ellen.

So when they had finished drinking their tea and eating their sandwiches, they took each others' hands.

'Right, let's close our eyes and concentrate very hard' said Katie.

As they were concentrating, it was as if they were dreaming, because they saw themselves standing in the mist and holding on to each others' hands. From a distance they could see some movement, but they weren't sure who it was. Eventually the mist began to disappear and Gail could see Dylan coming towards her with his fluffy white coat, his brown ears and his big brown eyes. He stood right in front of Gail, and then he was suddenly transformed into a young man. He had long brown hair and brown eyes and was wearing blue jeans and a blue shirt, and his face was quite pale.

'Hi Mum' he said.

'Dylan? Is that you?' said Gail.

'Yes Mum, it's me.' Katie was right, I was a person

in my past life and then I came back as a dog.'

'You certainly did Dylan, a stunning one. Tell me something, have I treated you all right?'

'You know you have Mum. I know life was so difficult for us, but now it's changed for the better.'

'Tell me something Dylan, would you like to go back to being a young man again?'

'No Mum, I love being a dog because I get all the attention and all the cuddles and kisses from all three of you.'

'Did you have a family in your past life?'

'No, I was an orphan. I basically had to look after myself.' Gail's eyes were full of tears.

'I never thought I would have a second chance of life, or for someone to love me. Even though I'm a dog I'm still a person inside. And the way I feel now Mum is that I've got something special at last, people who really love me. And the love will never stop.'

He went over to Gail and put his arms around her and held her tight. He could feel the tears from her eyes running down her cheeks and on to his shirt.

'It's OK Mum, I'm here.'

'I only wish I could have saved you in your past life.'

'I know Mum, but that's the way my life was, unfortunately. I love you Mum.'

'I love you too Dylan.'

Then Dylan let go. He approached Ellen and Katie and gave them both a hug, and then he went back and stood in the same place as when he had first arrived. Suddenly mist surrounded him, and he changed into a dog again. He ran up to Gail and jumped all over her, kissing her face.

'That was mind blowing' said Ellen.

'Yes it was' said Gail. 'Thank you Katie for making that happen, it was so special to see Dylan as a young man.'

'Thank *you* Gail, it was really down to you that he came.'

'What do you mean Katie?'

'Well, you wanted Dylan to show himself as a person, and for all the love you have for him in your heart, it was the love that brought him to you.'

'I feel so touched that he did that for me' said Gail.

Eventually they looked up to see Dylan sitting next to Gail with his head in her lap, looking straight into her eyes. Gail gave him a kiss and a big hug. Katie went into the kitchen and made some tea, and she put some whisky into the cups. She then brought the tea into the living room.

'I put some whisky in our tea, I hope you don't mind' said Katie.

'That's fine' said Ellen.

'I know I should be used to miracles by now, but that was a big one. I wasn't sure if something was going to actually happen.'

'It was just an idea, but as I said before you made it happen Gail,' said Katie. 'And for some strange reason I sort of knew that Dylan was once a person.'

They finished drinking their tea and Ellen turned to ask Gail if she was feeling OK, but she was asleep.

'I don't believe it Ellen, I didn't give her a lot of whisky in her tea' said Katie.

'Maybe it was the shock of seeing Dylan as a person' said Ellen.

'You're probably right' said Katie, and they both laughed. Ellen asked Katie if she wanted to have her tea leaves read.

'You read tea leaves Ellen?' asked Katie.

'I've been reading them for years.'

'How fascinating. OK, you can read my cup. I'll just go and make some more tea' said Katie.

Ten minutes later, Katie brought the tea into the living room. But when she started to drink it she made a funny expression.

'Ellen this tastes horrible.'

'I know Katie, the taste isn't very nice but it is worth it to have your tea leaves read.'

Katie finished drinking her tea and gave Ellen her cup. Ellen went through to the kitchen and went over to the sink and turned the cup upside down onto her hand, then turned it around three times. She then turned the cup the right way up and took it into the living room. She sat down on the sofa next to Katie and started looking at the tea leaves in the cup.

'What do you see?' asked Katie.

'I can see you standing, but not in this world, you are standing outside your home crying and I see smoke all around your house.'

'You can see that?'

'I also see you bending down at a gravestone, putting flowers next to it. That's in the other part of the cup. You've had such a hard life, and at one point you lost all your faith, this is all at the bottom of the cup. The top half is much better. You are sitting in your cottage feeling at ease with no worries or pressure any more. And you are much happier. I can see someone, right at the top of the cup. This may sound crazy, but the person has wings and her hands are reaching out to you and she is smiling. I think she is an angel looking out for you. The initial B is next to her.'

'This is amazing Ellen, that must be my mum.'

'What's her name?'

'It's Barbara.'

'Well she has been watching over you. She knows now that you have peace in your life and that makes her happy. Here, take your cup Katie, that's me done.'

'So what did you think of the reading?'

'I'm very impressed, you have a gift Ellen. I would love to be able to do that' said Katie.

'I'll tell you one thing Katie, that was a special cup reading.'

'Have you read others Ellen?'

'Quite a lot actually. I've done Gail's a few times. She loves getting her cup read.'

Gail eventually woke up. 'Did you enjoy your sleep?' asked Katie.

'Yes I did, sorry I dozed off, it must have been the alcohol. What was it you put in my tea Katie?'

'It was just a drop of whisky.'

'I'm surprised you're still awake Mum, you didn't even drink it all.'

'I know Gail, I reckon it's the excitement that's keeping me awake,' said Ellen.

'When you were asleep Gail, your mum read my tea leaves, and I thought it was incredible. The things she saw were quite amazing' said Katie.

60

'I can imagine, she's really good at it' said Gail. 'Mum, will you read my cup, just to see what it says? I don't expect you to do it just now, but in the next couple of days, if that's OK.'

'Of course it is' said Ellen.

'I think I'll go and make some soup for us,' said Katie.

'Do you need a hand?' asked Ellen.

'No you're OK Ellen, just you sit and relax.'

So a while later, Katie brought the soup into the living room on a tray.

'Oh great, I'm hungry' said Ellen.

Dylan got up from the chair and went over to Katie and barked as if to say, what about me?

'Don't worry Dylan, I've got something for you and Blacky and it's already made.' So Katie went back into the kitchen and put some macaroni into their bowls. Then she called to them and the dogs ran into the kitchen to get their dinner.

When the women had finished eating their soup, they went for a walk down to the ocean to see the dolphins. Gail closed her eyes and wished for a bench, and when she opened her eyes, there it was on the sand. They all sat down next to the ocean.

'I was just thinking Mum, would you like to go and see the animals?'

'That would be nice Gail. You know something Katie, ever since Gail was a child, she always loved animals and wanted to take them all in. Now she is actually doing it. It makes me very proud of her.' She smiled at Gail.

Now and again they would see the dolphins coming out of the water. After they had sat for a while, they went to see the dogs. As they were approaching the house, Ellen turned to Gail and asked who lived there.

'The dogs live there Mum.' Ellen looked at Gail and said, 'They must be the luckiest dogs in the world.'

'Well Mum, Katie and I saved them from cruelty. They deserve luxuries in their lives. There's a house for the cats too. Anyway Mum, lets go inside and you can see the dogs.'

When they went in, the dogs were all over them. They were healthy looking and their coats were shiny. Gail could see that they dogs were much more content.

'What do you think of the dogs Mum?'

'They're lovely, and good natured as well' said Ellen. So Gail and Katie gave all the dogs their dinner. 'I think I'll stay here at night sometimes to keep the dogs company' said Gail. 'I know they have each other, but they must still get lonely.'

'That's a good idea' said Katie. 'I will do it sometimes as well.'

They left the dogs and went to see the cats. The way the houses were situated the animals couldn't hurt themselves, everything was safe for them. The cats had a cat flap so they could go out and come back in when they felt like it. Some of them were in the garden sleeping. As they went into the house, the cats and kittens inside went up to Gail, Katie and Ellen and began purring loudly and rubbing themselves against their legs. Gail went into the kitchen and put some food into all their little bowls. Then she gave them some milk. She then went into the living room, where Katie and Ellen were.

'Well, that's the cats eating their dinner' said Gail. 'At least we know that by using our powers, we can see them and what they are doing, and they know that this is their home now.'

They sat with the cats for a while and gave them some attention and lots of love. Dylan was licking their little faces and the cats were loving it. They weren't even afraid of him. Later on, they left and went to see the seals. They had to walk quite a distance. When they reached them Ellen said 'Oh Gail, look at the seals, aren't they just beautiful! Do you know something Gail, I've never seen seals in real life, and now I'm standing here looking at them.'

Most of the seals were in the water and they were obviously enjoying it. Gail noticed that there were more baby seals, and it made her feel happy that no bad person could get near them.

'At least they are safe now,' said Ellen.

'I know mum.'

'Right, let's move on,' said Katie. So they went to see the bears. They could see some of them in the water cooling down from the heat of the sun, while others were climbing trees and wandering around. A couple of the little bears were trying to play with one of the adults, but he couldn't be bothered.

'Doesn't that amaze you Gail?'

'Those little bears are like children' said Ellen.'

After a while, Katie and Ellen decided to go home, so Gail went to check on the elephants. When she eventually got to them she could see most of them rolling around in the muddy water and absolutely loving it. The baby elephants were getting bigger.

'Come on Dylan, let's go and get you some dinner' she said. Dylan barked and jumped up on her and she made a fuss of him. 'Who's a good boy? Yes you are.' They walked towards the ocean and Gail called out to Precious and Lightning, and they talked back to her, as dolphins do. When she took her shoes off and went into the water the dolphins came right up to her and swam around her.

She could see more dolphins in the distance and it made her feel good to know that they were free. Dylan went into the water to join her. she was stroking the dolphins, there were so many of them now. Gail knew that there was total trust between them. They seemed to like Dylan too.

Later at Katie's, Gail and Katie drank a toast to all the animals they had saved.

'Who would believe a magical world like this actually exists' said Ellen.

'I still think sometimes I am dreaming,' said Gail. 'Even though I've been here for a while now. No one from our world would ever believe that such a place could actually be real.'

'Yes it is rather spectacular isn't it, and it deserves special people' said Ellen.

'Yes you're right Mum, and our names are in the book of magic, so we must be special.' They all knew how lucky they were to have been chosen for this dream world.

'Anyway one thing is for sure, it's only people that have such hard lives and have been to hell and back who can get into this world,' said Gail. 'Anyway, what time is it?'

'Half past eleven' said Ellen.

'We'd better go now Mum, it's past your bed time' said Gail, laughing.

'Very funny!' said Ellen.

'Right Katie, we'll probably see you tomorrow.'

'OK Gail, goodnight.'

As they were making their way back home Gail said 'Listen Mum, do you want to stay with me tonight, since it's your first night?'

'Yes I would like that Gail, everything is still a little strange to me.'

'I know it feels that way just now, but you'll be fine.'

They got to the cottage and went in.

'Well, what do you think Mum? Your home is really beautiful, isn't it?'

'Yes, everything is just the way I would have wanted it.'

'Would you like a cup of tea before you go to bed?'

'No thanks Gail, I just want to go to bed, I'm exhausted.'

'OK, I'll show you to your room.'

Gail opened the bedroom door for her mother and wished her good night. She decided to go to bed as well, and as usual Dylan lay beside her on the bed.

As Gail dreamed, she could see herself standing in a black hole. The strange thing was that the black hole was going round and round, and for some reason Gail couldn't seem to move, she just kept standing in the same place. She knew something was wrong and could also feel it.

Suddenly Gail could see a black figure at the other end of the dark hole. She could sense it was a man, and he was floating towards her wearing a black cloak. As he got closer to her a shiver went down Gail's back.

'Who are you?' asked Gail.

'Don't you know?' asked the man.

'How should I know?'

'Well you are psychic, aren't you?' said the man. Gail didn't answer. She just looked straight into his dark eyes. She could feel his power from him.

'Wait a minute, I've seen you in my dreams before' said Gail.

'Because you have strong powers, and I intend to have those powers,' said the man.

'Not a chance! They belong to me now.'

'I can make you have the worst nightmares you have ever experienced. 'You'll be begging me to stop them!' said the man.

'I don't care what you do, you have no chance of stealing my powers. And I know you want to destroy this magical world, and turn it into something evil. Why do you want to do that?'

'Because I can,' said the man. He then turned and started to float towards the bottom of the black hole. As he got further down the hole he called out, 'I will take over, I will take over, and you will be coming with me!'

Just then Gail woke up, the sweat pouring from her face. She lay for about ten minutes, then got up and went down to the kitchen to make herself a cup of lemon tea. She then sat down at the kitchen table looking out of her window. It was still light outside. Despite her powers, Gail was still nervous and she was wondering how she was going to tell her mum, since she had just arrived. And Katie. 'But maybe Katie already knew, since she was psychic,' Gail thought to herself. Most of the time Gail and Katie could read each others minds.

She was just thinking about White Angel when she heard someone call out her name. 'Gail it's me, White Angel, open the back door.'

Gail got up off the chair and opened the back door. White Angel was floating high up in the air. She started moving down towards Gail and finally her feet landed right in front of her.

'It's good to see you White Angel.'

'You too Gail. Are you OK?'

'Yes, I think so. I take it you know what just happened?'

'Yes I could see in your dreams. Don't worry Gail, our powers are strong and we are good decent people, which will help us. You see Gail, the good always wins in the end. We are all going to have to use our minds to fight, which will take a lot out of us, but we are strong enough for it. This is going to sound strange, but listen to what I'm saying to you. I'm in contact with the spirit world. They will be coming to help us when the time comes. It will give us more strength.'

'Do they have powers too?' asked Gail.

'Yes, you will be surprised at the powers they have. We are definitely not alone in this. We need their help because there is a lot of evil somewhere in the darkness out there.'

'Where are my manners? Come in White Angel' said Gail.

'No its OK, I need to go anyway, don't worry I'll be back very soon.'

Gail watched as she went up into the air and through the clouds until she couldn't see her any more. She closed the back door and made another cup of lemon tea for herself. She was a lot calmer after seeing White Angel.

'What a perfect name for a perfect angel,' Gail thought to herself. She took her tea into the living room and she put the television on. Even though she lived in a very different world, she could still tune in with her mind to get the television channels that she used to watch in her old life. Dylan came down the stairs and came straight into the living room to see her.

'Morning Dylan, who's a good boy?' she said. His tail was wagging and he licked her face. His eyes were looking straight at her as if to say he knew what was wrong.

'You know what's going on don't you Dylan? Maybe you dreamed it too' she said. Dylan barked. 'Do you want some breakfast Dylan?' He barked again as if to say OK. So she and Dylan went into the kitchen and she gave him some cereal. She then made a slice of toast for herself. She could hear her mother moving around upstairs, so she made tea and toast for her too. Ellen came downstairs and into the kitchen.

'Good morning Gail.'

'Morning Mum, did you sleep well?'

'You know something Gail, that was the best sleep I've had in ages. Maybe it's because life is stress free here.'

Not for long, Gail thought to herself.

'Here Mum, I've made you a cup of tea and some toast.'

'Thank you Gail, the tea is so fresh here, nothing like where we come from.'

'You're right Mum, it's delicious. Do you know something, you look so much healthier.'

'I know Gail, and I feel twenty years old again. Gail, is something wrong?'

'No Mum, I'm OK.'

'You don't seem your usual cheery self, you're usually so happy. It seems like you have a lot on your mind.'

'Stop worrying Mum, I'm really OK.' Gail didn't have the heart to tell her mum about the dream for now.

'It's a lovely day and everything seems so pure and clean and the sun is making everything shine, what a sight,' said Ellen.

Gail was trying to come up with solutions to help them. Suddenly she could hear Katie in her mind.

'Gail' she was saying, 'I know what's going on. I could hear you and White Angel talking through my mind. I'm worried too, but try not to put all the worry on yourself, it could weaken the strength and we can't afford to lose it. It took me a long time to get through to you, something must have been blocking us'

'I just don't know what, but at least I managed to get through to you somehow' said Katie. 'Come and see me soon Gail, today if you can.'

'I will Katie. Listen, what about my mum?'

'Bring her with you. We are going to have to tell her' said Katie.

'It's so unfair, she has just come here to stay' said Gail.

'I know, said Katie, I suppose it's just one of those things.'

'It makes me so angry Katie, she has been through enough as it is.'

'Listen Gail, Ellen is a lot stronger like me now and that will help a great deal' said Katie.

'What about Dylan, I'm scared for him? I don't know what I'd do if I lost him and the animals, they are really doing well now, but in a way I'm scared for them' said Gail, and her eyes were full of tears.

'Listen to me Gail, the devil and the demons will sense your weakness. You have got to try and stay strong. Think of Dylan.'

'I definitely will stay strong Katie for Dylan and the animals.'

'Right Gail, see you soon.'

'OK Katie.'

Ellen was calling out to Gail, 'Gail, can you hear me?' Although Gail's eyes were open, in a strange way she looked like she was asleep. As Ellen was trying to wake up Gail, she looked into her eyes. Suddenly Gail spoke.

'Are you OK Mum?'

'Gail, I've been trying to wake you up for ages. That was quite scary. What have you been doing?'

'What do you mean?'

'Well, one minute you were in a deep sleep and your eyes were wide open and then all of a sudden you were staring and spoke to me. It was really creepy.'

'Sorry mum, I didn't mean to frighten you.'

'That's OK Gail.'

'Do you want to come with me to see Katie, Mum?'

'Does she know we're coming?'

'Yes she does.'

'OK, let's go' said Ellen.

So they left and went along by the ocean to see the dolphins.

'Can you hear them speaking, Mum?' asked Gail.

'Yes I can, and I reckon they know it's you.'

'Yes, I actually think they do. After all, they are intelligent mammals.'

When they got to Katie's cottage the door opened as usual. Katie called to them to enter. She had made tea for them and a cake.

'Did you make the cake yourself Katie, or did you wish for it?' asked Gail.

'I made it myself for a change' said Katie. 'Just to see how it would taste. Right then, let's go into the living room.'

Once in the living room, Katie cut the cake into slices and gave Ellen the first two slices.

'This cake is delicious' said Ellen. Gail and Katie then took a couple of slices.

'I hope I don't get poisoned from eating this, Katie!' said Gail, laughing.

'Don't you be so cheeky!' said Katie, smiling at her.

When they had finished drinking their tea, Katie said to Ellen: 'Why don't you read Gail's tea leaves?'

Gail gave Katie a worried look. 'I'll read them if you want me to Gail.'

'It's OK Mum, you don't have to.'

'This is not like you Gail' said Ellen. 'You usually can't wait for me to read them.'

'I don't want to be a nuisance Mum.'

'You're not a nuisance. And anyway, it's been a while since I've read your tea leaves.'

'OK then Mum.'

Gail knew her mum wasn't going to give up, so Katie made the tea and took it through to the lounge. Ellen and Katie had normal tea. When Gail had finally finished her tea, she went into the kitchen, went over to the sink and turned the cup upside down on her left hand. Then she turned it round three times. Afterwards she went back into the living room and gave her mum the cup.

'OK Gail' Ellen said. 'Let's see what's in store for you. I can see you talking to someone. She's tall and is wearing a long dress and you seem to be talking about something important. There is something strange here.'

'What is it Mum?'

'Her feet don't touch the ground, and this happened recently. I sense that she is a very important person, and is dedicated to something massive, but I don't know what it is.'

Then she smiled and said: 'I see Dylan here, and he's right beside you Gail, and there are hundreds of animals all over your cup. I do sense how they had been badly treated, but now they are happy and content with their life. I can see the dolphins too. There are quite a lot of them. Oh what's this?'

'What is it mum?'

'I see a man standing and there are others behind him' said Ellen. 'Oh my God, I just got a shiver down my back. This is bad. There is a massive dark place. It's like a tunnel and it's turning round all the time. It's as if it's alive.'

'What do you mean? How can you tell it's turning?'

'I sense it Gail' said Ellen. 'I also see the starting of a fire. It might not come to anything, but if it does it will be bad. I see the initials W and A. Do you know who that could be?'

'Yes I think so mum', said Gail.

'The initials are near that woman I told you about. She is wearing a long dress. Do you remember me saying that to you Gail?'

'Yes, I do Mum.'

'Who is she?'

'She is someone very special, and her name is White Angel. Do you remember me and Katie talking about her?'

'Yes, I do. She's a witch, isn't she?'

'Yes, that's right mum.'

'I sense that she's a good witch', said Ellen.

'You're absolutely right Mum.'

'I feel that she is a leader and is very helpful, and I can see that she watches over you and Katie. Well that's me finished Gail. There's nothing else in your cup.'

'Thanks. Listen Mum, I've got to tell you something. White Angel came to see me this morning and she told me that there could possibly be a war. A while back we had talked about it and hoped that it wouldn't come to anything, and we were hoping that the demons would realize just how strong our powers were, and maybe they would back off. But it doesn't look like that's going to happen. We've got more power than they'll ever know.'

'What do you mean?'

'Well Mum, we'll be getting help from the spirit world.'

'You mean ghosts?'

'Yes Mum, and there will be hundreds of them. Just in case you're wondering, they're the good spirits that will help us. I know from the devil's world that they have evil spirits, but we have a lot more good spirits on our side, which makes us more powerful. I know it's a lot to take in mum. It's been a lot for us to take in as well. I'm so sorry. I know you have just arrived here.'

'It's OK Gail' said Ellen. 'It's not your fault. There are some things you can't control in life, and this is one of them. For some reason I know we will win.'

'What are you saying Mum? Do you want to be a part of this?'

'Of course I do Gail.'

'I thought maybe you would want to go back to your old life.'

'No, I want to stay and help fight for this beautiful, magical world', said Ellen. 'I'm definitely here for life.'

'You don't know how good it is to hear you say that mum.' Gail hugged her.

'I wonder what we will be up against' said Katie.

'We will just have to wait and see' said Gail. 'Do you know, it's strange. For years and years I've watched horror movies and now it's actually happening in real life. It's really quite scary.'

They all decided to go for a walk. Katie took little Blacky with her to give him some exercise.

'I've decided to stay with the dogs tonight to

give them some company' said Gail.

'Will you be OK Mum?'

'I'll be fine. I want to go to my own little cottage tonight and get settled in.'

'OK' said Gail. 'I want to show you something special Mum.'

So Gail and Katie took Ellen up to the waterfall.

'Well, what do you think Mum?'

'It's really spectacular and magical, and look at the gold running through the water' said Ellen. 'This is just paradise!'

'I took a shower in that waterfall' said Gail.

'You did?'

'Yes, but I had my bathing suit on', said Gail. 'It was amazing. The gold was all over my body and it was gleaming.'

'This is incredible' said Ellen. 'I've never seen a waterfall like this in all my life. This is definitely true magic.' She put her hands under the water and watched as the gold went all over them. She touched the gold and said: 'Wow, real gold. I can't believe I'm actually touching this.' She then put it back into the water where it belonged.

'Has this waterfall always been here?'

'I'm not sure mum. Can you tell us, Katie?'

'Yes, it has always been here. That was one thing nobody wished for. Nobody wished for the ocean either. So they have always been here. When you first came here to stay Gail, everything around us started to become real and the cartoon effect began to disappear. Now this world has come to life.'

'That is fascinating' said Ellen.

Gail then wished for a rug to sit on and a bowl of fruit, and immediately a rug appeared on the grass with a bowl of fruit on top of it. They sat on the rug and ate some of the fruit. Gail took some biscuits out of her pocket and gave them to Dylan and Blacky.

After they had all sat there for a while, they got up from the rug. As they started to walk away, the bowl and the rug vanished.

When they got back to Katie's, the sun was beginning to go down and stars were appearing in the sky. Katie asked them 'Do you two fancy some dinner?'

71

'That would be nice' said Gail. 'What about you mum? Would you like to stay for some dinner?'

'Yes I would' said Ellen.

'I've had a wonderful day Gail' said her mother.

'That's good Mum, and there will be many more wonderful days' said Gail. 'You can be sure of that.'

After giving Dylan and Blacky their food, Katie took Gail and Ellen's dinner through to the living room. 'Here we are' she said, 'Get stuck in girls.'

'Macaroni, my favourite' said Gail.

When they were finished, Ellen washed the dishes and dried them, Gail made some coffee and then they both went back into the living room.

'I'm just wondering' said Ellen, 'will I be able to wish for things quite soon?'

'Yes, mum. It won't be long before you see White Angel, and that's when things will happen. Unexpected things. You just have to be patient.'

'Well, it's time for me to go. I'm going to spend the night with the dogs', said Gail. 'Mum, do you want me to walk you back to your cottage now?'

'No, it's OK Gail. I'll go in a little while.'

'Listen Ellen, if you want, I'LL walk you back to the cottage. I've got to take Blacky out anyway' said Katie.

'Thanks Katie, that would be really good of you. I just like to know that my mum's OK. Even though you're in the safest place in the world Mum, which you are, you've got to remember that there is a bad force out there. Even though they are far away and in another world, it won't stop them from trying to get closer to us in our minds. They will know you are quite vulnerable just now. Even I can sense it'

'Well you don't have to worry Gail. Katie is going to walk me home. So on you go, before it gets any later.'

'OK Mum, see you tomorrow.' 'Goodnight Katie.'

'Goodnight Gail.'

Gail and Dylan went to the dogs' house, and when Gail opened the door, the dogs were all over her. She gave them all big hugs, then went into the kitchen and gave them all some dinner. She then put the kettle on and made herself a cup of lemon tea. Then she put the television on and lay on the sofa. Dylan jumped up and lay beside her. She knew he was a little jealous of the other dogs.

'You're my boy, aren't you Dylan' she said. 'Don't worry, you're my favourite.' He gave her a paw and licked her face.

Some of the other dogs came into the lounge and lay beside the sofa next to Gail. One of them kept licking her hand. When she had finished drinking her tea, she played with the dogs for a while, throwing their squeaky toys for them. They were having so much fun.

After playing for a while, the dogs fell asleep. Gail lay on the sofa with Dylan beside her and they both slept.

It was morning before Gail woke up. She had to wake up Dylan so that she could move. 'Come on Dylan. I'LL make you some breakfast.' He jumped off the sofa with his tail wagging. The rest of the dogs were still asleep.

'That's strange' Gail thought to herself. Usually if she asked Dylan if he wanted breakfast, he would bark. He must have known not to wake up the other dogs.

Gail made a cup of lemon tea for herself and made Dylan some toast. Then she opened the back door for some fresh air. She sat down at the kitchen table and drank her tea.

Dylan went out the back and walked around in the garden. The sun was so bright that it made his white coat shine. Gail made another cup of lemon tea and went out into the garden. She sat down in one of the chairs and basked in the sun for a while. The sun was lovely and warm.

She hoped days like this would last forever, but a fear did cross her mind that one day all the beauty in this world could be gone. She felt a shiver down her back. She knew that if the place was destroyed, she would probably die too. Even if she didn't die, her heart would definitely be dead. So for her there would no longer be any point in living.

Some of the dogs came out the back door looking for her. She called to them and they went over to her, and she made a fuss of them. After sitting for a while, she got up from the chair and went into the house and gave all the dogs their breakfast. The dogs could come and go when they wanted, because on both doors there were massive cat flaps big enough for the dogs to get through.

When the dogs had finished their breakfast, Gail took them all for a walk.

There were so many of them, small dogs, large dogs and medium sized. She took them down to the ocean, and most of them went in for a swim. But Dylan stayed right beside Gail. He wouldn't leave her side. Gail had about ten puppies all around her and they were all on leashes. They were nearly tripping her up.

Then she heard Katie call her, and turned around.

'Hi Gail, aren't you busy!' she said, and laughed.

Katie had little Blacky with her.

'Hi Katie, I wanted to give the dogs a special treat' said Gail.

'Look at them swimming in the water. They're loving it' said Katie. 'Is your mum still in bed?'

'I don't know, I've not seen her yet.'

'Would you like me to go and see how she is?'

'That would be great' said Gail.

So Katie lifted up Blacky and went to Ellen's cottage. When she got there, she knocked on the door and Ellen opened it.

'Hello Ellen, I thought I would come and see how you are' Katie said.

'I'm fine' said Ellen.

'Did you sleep well?

'Yes I had a great sleep.'

'Gail's down at the ocean with all the dogs' said Katie.

'All of them?'

Katie nodded. 'You know what she's like Ellen. She wanted to give them a big treat. You should come down and see for yourself.'

Down at the ocean, Ellen asked her daughter how she was coping.

'I'm doing fine mum. In fact, I'm loving all of this' Gail said.

'I think Dylan's a little jealous' said Ellen.

'Yes mum. He's not left my side since we've been here. I've been giving him a lot of attention and trying to make him feel better' said Gail.

Ellen decided to take the pups from Gail to give her a break.

'Thank you mum. My hands can have a rest now' said Gail. Ellen took the puppies to the edge of the water and splashed the water all over them. They were trying to catch the water with their mouths. Ellen couldn't help but laugh at them, because it was quite funny to watch. Gail took her sandals off and went into the water with Dylan. The water was clear and gleaming from the sun. She only went in so far, because Dylan was very wary of the water, so she stayed right beside him to make sure he was all right. 'You're a lovely boy, aren't you Dylan?' said Gail and he licked her face.

A while later she took Dylan out of the water and he gave himself a shake. They then went over to join Katie and Ellen. Gail took the puppies from Ellen and said: 'Thanks for looking after them for me.'

'You're welcome' her mother said. They all sat on the beach for a while looking at the ocean.

'This is just paradise, isn't it mum?' Gail said.

'It sure is' said Ellen.

A couple of hours later Gail decided to take the dogs back home. When they finally got back to the house, Gail gave them all something to eat and stayed for a while. As she sat in the lounge, she closed her eyes and put her hand across her forehead and mentally checked all the animals. It was as if she was turning one channel over and then another. They all seemed to be doing fine. She opened her eyes, content that the animals were all right.

A while later she went to see how the cats were doing. As she reached the house, some of them were lying in the garden. A couple of them went over to Gail and purred at her. She bent down and stroked them, then went into the house. The other cats were all over Gail and they seemed to like Dylan too. Dylan was so good with other animals, but sometimes when the animals approached Gail, he got very jealous.

Gail went into the kitchen and gave the cats and the kittens their dinner and some milk. They all loved milk.

As Gail played with them, she noticed that the kittens were getting bigger. She knew she didn't need to worry about them because the older cats looked after them as they do in the wild. She could always check with her mind anyway, just to make sure they were all right.

One of the kittens, black with a white chest, went up to Gail, jumped up on her lap and got comfortable. She started purring quite

loudly. Gail stroked her and said: 'You are beautiful, aren't you?'
The kitten looked up at her in agreement and kept purring.

Dylan started licking Gail's hand and then barked a couple of
times. 'It's OK Dylan. You're my number one dog and I love you' said
Gail. She then cuddled him. He lay down and put his front paws over
her sandals and went to sleep. She stroked his head with one hand and
used her other hand to stroke the kitten. Eventually she fell asleep.

Meanwhile, Ellen and Katie were sitting in Katie's living room watching
television and relaxing. Little Blacky lay beside Katie on the chair.

'I wonder what's taking Gail so long' said Ellen.

'She'll be making sure the animals are OK', said Katie. 'At least she doesn't
have to go and check on the animals every day, so she can have a break sometimes.'

Just then Gail and Dylan came into the living room and
Ellen noticed that Gail was holding a little kitten.

'She kept following me' Gail explained. 'She wouldn't
leave me alone. I think she's attached herself to me.'

'So have you adopted her?' asked Ellen.

'I don't know yet. I've got to think about Dylan. I might keep her for
a while since she's so little. When I was at the cats' house, she came up to
me and sat on my lap and wouldn't budge. Eventually when I lifted her
and put her on the floor, she kept going around my legs and meowing
really loud as if she was crying. I couldn't leave her there like that. So I
took her with me. I suppose I'm just a soft touch at heart' said Gail.

'There's nothing wrong with that' said Katie. 'I'll go
and make you a nice cup of lemon tea Gail.'

'Thanks Katie.' Gail started yawning.

'Are you tired Gail? said her mum.

'Just a little, Mum' said Gail.

Ellen tried to take the kitten, but it wouldn't let go of
Gail. Dylan seemed sad as he lay next to Gail.

'Dylan, who's my favourite boy?' said Gail and stroked
him. Dylan just lay there with his tail wagging.

Katie brought the tea through to the living room

'Here's your lemon tea Gail' she said. 'I made ordinary tea for us, Ellen.'

'Thanks Katie. I'll enjoy this', said Gail.

'Won't the kitten let go?' asked Katie.

'No, it's like she's stuck to me' said Gail.

'She obviously took to you' said Katie. 'Are the dogs OK Gail?'

'Yes, they're fine, and all the other animals are doing fine as well.'

Ellen and Gail stayed at Katie's for dinner, and afterwards Katie and little Blacky went to spend the night with the dogs. Ellen, Gail, Dylan and the little kitten went home. As they got to Gail's cottage, Gail said: 'Mum, are you coming in or are you going to your own cottage?'

'I think I'll go back' said Ellen. 'I'm still trying to settle in.' So Gail walked her mum to her cottage. 'Right Mum' she said. 'I'll see you tomorrow. Goodnight.'

'Goodnight Gail' her mother replied.

Back at Gail's cottage, the kitten let go of her. It was as if she knew that this was her new home. So Gail put her down and opened the door and they went inside. Gail then wished for some food for the kitten, and when she went into the kitchen and opened the cupboards, there it was. She put some food out for the kitten and gave Dylan his dinner. He kept watching the kitten.

'Come on Dylan, eat your dinner' said Gail, and she stroked him and gave him a cuddle.

Gail felt guilty for bringing a new animal into their home, because it had always been just Dylan and her. She knew Dylan wouldn't be too happy. She closed her eyes and wished for a new toy for him. As she opened her eyes, a squeaky toy appeared right in front of her floating in the air. She got a hold of it and said: 'Here you are Dylan.'

His tail was wagging and he started barking, so she threw the ball for him a few times. He seemed a lot happier.

Afterwards she made a mug of hot chocolate for herself and sat in the living room to relax for a while. The kitten came through to the living room meowing and looking for her.

'It's OK, I'm here' she said, lifting the kitten up and putting

it beside her. Dylan lay on the sofa next to Gail and put his
head on her stomach. Eventually they all fell asleep.

Gail woke up the next morning with Dylan's nose on her chin
and the kitten on her chest. She stroked them, and the kitten woke
up and let out a big yawn. She lifted the kitten on to the carpet
and said: 'Come on Dylan. Let's go and get breakfast.'

After breakfast, Gail opened the back door to let Dylan out and the kitten
followed him. Gail took her tea and went out to join them. She sat on the white
bench and watched them. The kitten was trying to play with Dylan, but Dylan still
wasn't sure of her. He needed time to get used to her. The kitten went over to Gail,
and she lifted her up and said: 'What are you doing? Are you annoying Dylan?'

The kitten just looked at Gail and said: 'Meow.'

Gail then put her on the bench beside her and said: 'There's a
good girl. We will have to think of a name for you, won't we?' The
kitten just looked at her with her big green eyes. Dylan then went
up to Gail and licked her hand. Gail gave him a cuddle.

Then she heard a knock on her front door. She got up from the
bench and went round to the front of the cottage. It was her mum.

'Hi Gail!'

'Morning mum! Did you sleep well?'

'Yes I did. I was really tired for some reason. What
about you, did you have a good sleep?'

'Yes, I did. Dylan, the kitten and I all fell fast asleep on the sofa.'

'How is the kitten getting on?'

'She's fine mum. She's round the back. Come and see her sitting there.'

'She is so cute, isn't she?' said Ellen. 'Have you decided on a name for her yet?'

'No mum. I'm thinking of one.' Gail brought out the tea. 'So
mum. How are you enjoying staying at your new cottage?'

'I love it Gail.'

'Do you miss your old house?' asked Gail.

'No, not at all. This is heaven compared to where I used to be' said Ellen.

'I take it that you don't miss the old world Gail?'

'No Mum, I've never been happier. It's amazing how a dream can change your life forever.'

'I take it you didn't see demons in your dreams last night?'

'No Mum, I had a nice peaceful sleep. I don't even remember dreaming. Every night when I'm just about to go to sleep, I wonder if the demons, or the devil for that matter, is going to come into my dreams. But I stay strong in my mind because I know I have to. Have you had any strange dreams?'

'No, not like your dreams anyway Gail. I did dream of you when you were a baby. You were just born and it was like my world was repeating itself again. Like I was still twenty eight years old. When I woke up, I could have sworn I saw you in my arms as a baby again. Then something made me look into the mirror and I saw...' She stopped.

'Tell me mum, what did you see?' asked Gail.

'I saw myself holding you, and I was twenty eight again. Then I noticed someone behind me in the mirror and I had a feeling it was a man. He was wearing a black hooded cloak, and as he moved from behind me I could see his black eyes staring at me in the mirror. His face was a reddish colour. I just froze. I couldn't move. I just lay there in my bed and kept watching. The next thing I saw blood coming from your eyes and running down your cheeks. I screamed and got out of bed and went towards the mirror and shouted that it was not real. Then suddenly it all stopped. As I looked in the mirror, I was never so glad to see my own reflection again. It was strange seeing myself and being that young again and holding you Gail. I got shivers right down my back.'

'When did you have that dream Mum?'

'I had it the first night I was here.'

'Why didn't you say anything?'

'Well, I just thought I must have been dreaming all the way through and put it down to a bad dream. 'I've been trying to forget about it, but it was so real.'

Gail had a feeling that the dream meant something bad, but she didn't know what.

'Do me a favour Mum' she said. 'If you have a bad dream or anything like that happens again, please tell me. I want to know, OK?'

'All right Gail' said Ellen. 'You look worried. What is it?'

'It's OK. I've just got to figure this out, and I will.'

Gail suddenly felt a cold sensation going through her body, but she wasn't sure if it was good or bad. 'Hopefully good' she thought to herself. Then she saw a vision. The ocean turned black, a cold, cold blackness. The sand wasn't gold any more but had turned a grey colour. The vision was gone, just as quick as it had come. She was in shock for a few minutes before she finally snapped out of it.

'I need a drink of water Mum' she said.

'OK Gail, I'll get you one' said Ellen. She came back outside with the glass of water and handed it to her daughter.

'Thanks Mum' said Gail, and drank all the water.

'Are you OK now Gail?'

'Yes Mum, I'm all right, but I've got to see White Angel as soon as possible, and it will need to be today or tonight even. I know something's going to happen soon.'

'How soon?

'I reckon it will be within the next couple of weeks. We've got to start making plans.'

She lifted up the kitten and called to Dylan, and they all went back inside the cottage and sat down in the living room. As usual, Dylan sat next to Gail and the kitten lay on her lap. Gail looked at the time. It was one fifteen in the afternoon. Suddenly, she could hear White Angel calling to her in her mind.

'The war is coming soon Gail and we need to be prepared. And you were right Gail. It is going to happen in the next couple of weeks.'

'Are you getting closer White Angel, because I think I can sense it?' Gail asked.

'Yes I am Gail. I'm at the front door' replied White Angel.

Gail got up from the chair and went to the door and opened it to let White Angel in. Gail took her through to the living room and said: 'Mum, I'd like you to meet White Angel.'

Ellen shook White Angel's hand. 'It's a pleasure to meet you' she said. 'And it's a pleasure to meet you too Ellen' replied White Angel.

Dylan approached White Angel and licked her hand, and she stroked him and smiled.

'I spoke to the spirit world last night and they said that when war begins, they will know and they will join us' said White Angel.

'What kind of weapon will we be using?' asked Gail.

'We won't be using a weapon Gail. We will be using our minds, because that is where the powers are, as you know.'

Gail's eyes were full of tears, and as one tear fell on to her hand, she noticed that it was black.

'What is this?' she asked.

'This is a bad sign' said White Angel.

'What do you mean?'

'I think they are going to take you over. In fact, I'm sure of it. Remember when your mum had a bad dream?'

Ellen just looked at White Angel, surprised.

'Gail, going back to when you were a child, you sensed something was wrong, didn't you?'

'Yes I did' said Gail.

'The devil and the demons were there in your head. It's only coming to the surface now because you're in our precious world.'

'Why me though?'

'Because you can be too soft and vulnerable, and that's a sign of weakness. But your heart and the special powers you have always had saved you from the devil and the demons.'

'Oh my God. I can't believe this' said Gail.

'Well it's true, and now they've come back for more. It was just unfortunate that I couldn't take you when you were younger. It was the same for Katie too, and of course your mum, but I had to wait until you were older and had more power. I know you and Dylan had a hard time, and I would like to say that I and the spirit world are sorry about that. Let me put my hands on your head Gail.'

White Angel touched Gail's head with her hands and said: 'Now close your eyes and concentrate.' The cottage started shaking and a bolt of lightning came from the sky and right through Gail's roof, leaving a massive hole. It then struck Gail's head.

The whole place was glowing. It lasted for perhaps ten seconds, and then White Angel took her hands away slowly. Sparks were flying from all over her. 'Now Gail, open your eyes slowly. How do you feel?'

'I'm a little dazed, but apart from that I'm fine.'

'Does your head hurt at all?' asked White Angel.

'No, it doesn't.'

'Didn't you feel anything Gail?' said Ellen.

'No, not a thing Mum', said Gail. 'Why? What happened? Why is there a hole in my roof?'

'It's OK Gail. I can fix that. Don't worry' said White Angel. 'You just had a blow to the head from a bolt of lightning.'

'Why didn't she feel anything?' asked Ellen.

'In a way it's like she is programmed for it. Like being tuned in so that she won't feel pain.'

'That is amazing!'

'Yes, I suppose it is. Now listen Gail. You're a witch like me now. You have great powers and you're stronger than before. Clasp your hands together tightly.'

Gail did so, and suddenly blue sparks flew from her hands.

'Oh my God! Did that really happen?' asked Gail.

'Yes it did Gail' said White Angel.

'I just got some feeling through my body there. I was hot all over and it was an overwhelming feeling.'

'Well, you're just like me now Gail' said White Angel.

'Thank you for this new gift you have given me.'

'You're welcome. I've got to go now, but I will see you soon.' As she went to leave, she turned to Gail and said: 'I don't want you to worry about the animals. We'll make sure they are all right. After all they are our first priority. We can put a see-through shield around them and that will keep them safe.'

'That sounds like a great idea', said Gail. 'I feel so relieved to know that the animals will be OK.'

'Anyway Gail, I'd better go now.' She said goodbye to them and left. Ellen and Gail stood at the front door to wave goodbye, and they watched her fly up towards the sky.

'Where do you think she's going Gail?'

'To do things that need to be done' Gail replied.

'I'm just thinking. You'll probably be able to fly now. That will be so much fun', said Ellen.

'Yes I reckon it will be and I've always wanted to fly like a bird' said Gail.

So she went outside, closed her eyes and thought about flying. Suddenly her feet lifted and when she opened her eyes, she saw that she was high in the air. Dylan started barking and was trying to jump up towards her.

'No Dylan, it's OK.' She landed her feet back on the ground.

'Was that good Gail?'

'Yes Mum, I really enjoyed it.'

Dylan ran up to Gail all excited and still barking.

'You're my boy, aren't you Dylan?' said Gail.

They went back inside the cottage.

'Where is the kitten mum?'

'She's in her little bed beside the sofa.'

Gail went to check on her and found her sound asleep.

Ellen went through to the kitchen to make some tea and toast. When she was done making it, she put the tea and the toast on to a tray and took it into the living room.

'I was just thinking, Mum' said Gail. 'I feel more confident now since I have been given more powers. I know I will be able to protect all of us.'

Just then there was a knock on the door. Gail opened it to find Katie standing there.

'Come in Katie. How are the dogs?'

'They're fine Gail. I had a great time with them last night and I gave them all something to eat before I left.'

'We can take turns in looking after them.'

'Yes, that's fine with me Gail.'

'Would you like a tea or coffee?' asked Gail.

'Yes tea would be great', said Katie.

As Gail made the tea, Dylan and the kitten kept following

her around hoping for something to eat, so Gail gave them both some treats before going through to the living room.

'Ellen was just telling me what had happened with you and White Angel' said Katie. 'That must have been amazing.'

'Well to be perfectly honest Katie, I didn't feel anything apart from a warmth all over my body' said Gail.

'So I take it you have more powers now?'

*Yes, I'm just like White Angel now.'

'That's great Gail. I'm pleased for you. So I take it we are going to have a hard time of it with this war?'

'Well it's not going to be easy mum. We will need to prepare ourselves, but we all know in our hearts that good can overcome evil.'

'Look - the roof is fixing itself!' said Ellen.

'So it is. Although it doesn't rain here and I'm thankful for that' said Gail.

'But what about the flowers and the trees, they need rain?'

'It's OK Mum. You see they are protected by a very special moisture which is always on them, so they are always wet. They won't die, and we would never let them anyway.'

'I understand' said Ellen.

Later that afternoon Gail made home-made soup herself, instead of wishing for it, and they all agreed it was delicious. After washing the dishes and making a pot of coffee for them, she closed her eyes and wished for a lemon cake. Seconds later she opened her eyes to see the cake on the kitchen table.

'It's amazing how you can do that Gail', said Ellen.

When they had finished drinking their coffee, they all decided to go for a walk. 'Come on Dylan', said Gail. 'You're going to have a wash in the ocean.'

Dylan was growling as if to say 'No chance'. He didn't like getting washed. In fact he hated it.

Down on the shore, Katie put Blacky in the water.

'Look Dylan. Blacky loves the water', said Gail.

But Dylan wasn't moving. He just stood there on the sand. Gail threw his ball into the water, but Dylan wasn't falling for that. He was a very intelligent dog.

So Gail tried another way. She put some chocolate on the sand near the water and when Dylan went towards the chocolate, Gail used her mind and moved the chocolate into the water. So Dylan went further into the water and eventually got hold of the chocolate. Gail then took her shoes off, rolled her jeans up and went into the water to wash him down.

'There's a good boy Dylan. It's not that bad getting a wash, is it? she said to him. Dylan let out a couple of growls as if he was answering her back. 'Who's a cheeky boy?' said Gail. He growled back again. Gail just smiled at him.

When she was done washing him, Dylan got out of the water and started shaking himself. The drops were going all over Ellen and Katie.

'You're a lovely boy, aren't you Dylan?' said Ellen. Dylan went straight over to Ellen, wagging his tail and licking her hand. When Gail got out of the water she said: 'Katie, look at Blacky's coat, it's so shiny.'

'I know. He looks as though he's had a polish' said Katie and they all laughed.

Then they saw the dolphins approaching the surface.

'Look!' said Ellen, 'the dolphins are here.'

'Hi Precious, hi Lightning' said Gail. Blue and Pepper were right behind them.

'That's their babies Mum. Aren't they just beautiful? They are so innocent and so very special. It's so sad how these beautiful creatures are captured from the wild and taken into a life of captivity for human entertainment. It's just so cruel when they should be free like in this in the big ocean' said Gail.

'I agree' said Ellen.

'Me too' said Katie.

'It's like these people don't have a conscience. They exploit these dolphins for money. We should try and save more. I'm sure there are a lot more dolphins that need to be saved.'

'At least the dolphins here are happy and they're doing fine, which is great to see', said Ellen.

They wandered towards the forest trees. As Dylan went into the woods, Blacky chased after him, trying to play. Gail put her hand across her face and closed her eyes to check on all the animals. The animals she saw first were the bears. They seemed to be enjoying life. Gail was so happy to see this, because the bears had a terrible life before they came to this magical world. The live picture then switched to the seals. One of the seals had given birth to three baby seals. They were white just like their mother, and also beautiful. Gail checked on all the other animals and they also were doing fine.

'At least now they don't have to fear anyone hurting them ever again and at the end of the day, they deserved respect just like us', Gail thought to herself.

She then opened her eyes.

'Is everything OK Gail?' said Katie.

'Yes, all the animals are fine', said Gail.

'Where is the kitten Gail, I've just noticed she isn't with us?' said Katie.

'I left her in the cottage, but I'm keeping an eye on her through my mind. She seems to be OK. I left food and milk out for her, which she has already eaten and drunk. Anyway, it's time to go back home.'

They all made their way back home. Eventually they reached Katie's cottage.

'Well, goodnight Gail.'

'Goodnight Ellen. I'll probably see you both tomorrow' said Katie.

'You will Katie' said Gail.

Gail and Ellen made their way back to Gail's cottage.

'It's beautiful here at night, isn't it Gail, and peaceful too?'

'Yes Mum, it is.'

'Are you coming in Mum?'

'OK Gail, I'll come in for a cup of tea.'

'Come on Dylan. I'll make you some dinner' said Gail.

Dylan barked and wagged his tail and they went into the cottage. Gail went through to the kitchen and put the kettle on and made the tea. Then she put some food out for Dylan and the kitten.

Gail could hear the kitten meowing in the hallway, so she went out into the hallway and lifted her up.

'Who's my girl?' 'Have you been good?'

'Have you decided on a name for her yet Gail?'

'No, I haven't mum, but I'll need to think of one soon.'

Gail gave the kitten a kiss and a cuddle and it licked her cheek. She put her back down on the floor and the kitten went to get her dinner. Gail sat down at the kitchen table and finished drinking her tea.

'Listen Gail, I know you have a lot on your mind but try not to worry, OK?' said Ellen.

'I'll try not to Mum. I just don't know how things are going to turn out' said Gail.

'Well I have a good feeling that everything will turn out OK.'

'I hope you're right Mum.'

After Ellen had gone, Gail decided to go to bed. She picked up the kitten. and called to Dylan.'

'I think I'll call you Lucky' she said to the little cat. 'What do you think? Do you like that name?'

The kitten was purring loudly. She put her into her cat bed, which was right beside Gail's. Dylan jumped up on to Gail's bed and lay close beside Gail with his head on the pillow. Gail knew he was feeling insecure. Eventually they all fell asleep.

As Gail was dreaming, she saw herself floating towards the sky. Someone was in front of her and even though the figure was high up in the air, it was so still that it scared Gail. As she floated further towards the person, she could sense it was a man. He was wearing a red hooded cloak. He held out his arms and was holding a baby.

'What are you doing?' said Gail.

'Take a good look' he said in a deep, evil voice.

Gail went closer to him. She looked at his black eyes to see that they were turning red.

'This baby is you Gail, and if I drop you, you will die. If you want to live, you will hand over this world to me.'

'No chance, I would rather die than give you this wonderful world' said Gail. 'Do you hear me?'

'We've been watching you ever since you were a child, but you know that don't you Gail?'

'Why do you want to destroy this wonderful place?' asked Gail. 'Haven't you got enough evil in your own world?'

'We take. That's what we do.'

He then let go of the baby. Gail moved faster than a bolt of lightning to catch her. She caught her just before she touched the ground.

'It's OK' she said to the baby, looking at her and knowing it was herself. The baby smiled at her and put her little hand on her cheek.

Gail closed her eyes for a few minutes. When she opened them again, the baby was gone as if it had never happened. She closed her eyes again and after a few seconds, she opened them to see that she was back in her room and still in her bed.

Sweat was pouring from her and the sheets were soaked - even the pillow was saturated. She was so glad that the dream was over.

She got up and went into the bathroom for a shower. Then she went down the stairs to the kitchen to make a cup of lemon tea. She stood at the window looking at the stars; one by one they were disappearing as it started to get light outside. She didn't really want to go back to sleep even though she was tired.

Then she heard Dylan coming down the stairs, so she called out to him and he came into the kitchen to see her.

'Who's a good boy, Dylan?'

'Woof woof' he replied, as if to say that he was.

Gail looked at the time; seven forty five in the morning. She gave Dylan some cornflakes and then made herself another cup of lemon tea and a slice of toast. She then went through to the living room and put the television on and sat down on the sofa. A cartoon was on.

Strange, she thought to herself, it had been like a cartoon when she had first arrived. Now everything was real.

Dylan went into the living room.

'Hi Dylan, was that good?' said Gail.

He barked and licked his lips. Gail cuddled him, then she got up from the sofa, went through to the kitchen and opened the back door to let him out. She then went upstairs to check on Lucky, who was still sleeping in her little bed. She went back down the stairs and out into the back garden. Dylan was lying on the grass. Gail sat on her white bench and noticed that there were a lot more white roses in the garden this morning. She just loved white.

Gail sat in the sun for a good while before getting up from the
bench and going to check on Lucky again. Dylan followed her.

'Hi Lucky', Gail said. 'You've been sleeping forever, haven't you?'

She picked her up and said: 'Come on Lucky, let's go
down the stairs and I'll give you your breakfast.'

Lucky was purring and putting her little head against Gail's cheek. Gail got
to the bottom of the stairs with Dylan right behind her and went through to
the kitchen. She put Lucky down on the floor and then got her food out of the
cupboard. She put some of the kitty food into her dish, then gave her some milk as
well. She then decided to do some housework. When she was finished cleaning, she
started vacuuming the carpets. Dylan hated the Hoover. He was trying to bite it.

'Dylan, that's enough', said Gail. She was trying not to laugh.

Once she was finally done she decided to go to her mum's. She lifted
Lucky up and said: 'Come on Dylan, let's go and see mum.' So they left and
went to Ellen's cottage. Gail knocked on the door and Ellen opened it.

'Hi Gail, come into the kitchen and I'll make a
cup of tea for us. Have you had breakfast?'

'Yes mum.'

'Did you sleep OK?'

'No, not really' Gail said. 'I had a bad dream, or maybe
I should say that it was real. Anyway I've been up for quite a
few hours now. I couldn't face going back to bed.'

'Why, what happened?'

'I was flying into the sky when I saw someone in front of me, a man, or
should I say the devil' Gail said. 'He was wearing a red hooded cloak and holding
a baby, and Mum, the baby was me. He was threatening to drop me if I didn't
give him this world, but I told him he had no chance. Then he dropped me,
but I moved like a rocket and caught her before she reached the bottom.'

'Oh my god Gail!' Ellen said. 'That must have been terrifying for you.
And really weird seeing yourself as a baby and holding yourself.'

'It was, Mum. When I was holding her, she smiled at me and put her little
hand on my face and then I closed my eyes and minutes later when I opened

them, she was gone, like she never had been there. It was so spooky. '

'That definitely is spooky' said Ellen. 'Here, drink your
tea Gail, or do you want something stronger?'

'No thanks mum. Tea is fine.'

'How is the kitten settling in?'

'Just fine. I think she loves her new home and I think Dylan is getting used
to her now. I forgot to tell you Mum, I named her. I'm calling her Lucky.'

'That's a lovely name Gail. Can I hold her?'

'Yes, if you can manage to get her off me. 5he's holding on real tight.'

Eventually Ellen managed to release her from Gail 'Hi Lucky,
who's a lovely girl? Yes you are' she said. 'Do you want some
milk? Listen Mum, just give her a little drop of milk.'

'It's good that Dylan's accepted her, isn't it Gail?'

'Yes mum, it is' said Gail. 'It's strange though, all those years it was
just me and Dylan and now we have a new member of the family.'

'Well you couldn't not take her and she obviously
took to you' said Ellen. 'It must have been fate.'

'Yes you're probably right mum' said Gail.

'Hey guess what Gail. When I woke up this morning and looked
out my kitchen window, I noticed there was a dolphin waterfall out in
my back garden and I could have sworn they moved for real.'

'It would have been real Mum.'

'What do you mean?'

'Well the same thing happened to me when I first came here to live. So I
freed the dolphins. I used my mind to release them from the waterfall. They
were floating in the air and went towards the ocean, and then I used my mind
to move them slowly into the water and they were free. Even though the
dolphins were on a waterfall, they are still alive and should be set free Mum.'

'I understand Gail. And you're right, we should release them.'

So Gail went out into the back garden and walked towards the
waterfall. She closed her eyes and used her mind to remove the dolphins
from the waterfall, and within seconds the two dolphins had removed

themselves. Ellen was standing at the kitchen window watching.

Gail then started walking towards the ocean. The two dolphins were floating in the air and were both right behind Gail. When she got to the ocean, she released them slowly into the water.

The dolphins loved it. A while later, they both came up to the surface of the water and let out an amazing sound. They looked at Gail as if to thank her for setting them free. She smiled at them and they disappeared deep into the ocean. Gail then went back to her mother's cottage, where she walked round to the back door and called out to her mum.

'I'm just coming Gail', said Ellen. Gail sat down on one of the chairs in the garden and then Ellen came out of the back door holding Lucky, with Dylan right behind her.

'Hi Gail, I was just finishing my housework.'

'Well Mum, that's the dolphins free now.'

'That's great Gail. Do you know I couldn't believe what I was seeing. It was incredible. You actually used your mind to remove those dolphins?'

'Yes, I did, didn't I?' said Gail. 'Sometimes I still can't believe I can do these things.'

'I was just wondering Gail...'

'What's that Mum?'

'Will I be able to have my dolphins replaced?'

'Yes Mum, you can still have dolphins, but they won't be real. They'll just be ordinary dolphins.'

'Ordinary dolphins will just be as good' said Ellen.

So Gail closed her eyes and wished very hard for two dolphins. A few seconds later, she opened her eyes and saw two dolphins on the waterfall. Then all of a sudden the water started running from it.

'Well, what do you think Mum? Do you like it?'

'I love it Gail. It's absolutely beautiful.'

Dylan was trying to get a drink from the waterfall, so she put some water in her hands and gave it to him.

Little Lucky was being nosy and looking all around the

waterfall. Gail lifted her and gave her a drink too.

'I'm just wondering where Katie is', Ellen said. 'We've not seen her so far today. I hope she's OK.'

'She'll be fine Mum', said Gail. 'I would know if she wasn't.'

'Let's go and visit her' said Ellen.

So they left the cottage and went to Katie's.

'Do you want me to take Lucky, Gail?' asked Ellen.

'No you're OK Mum, I'll hold her.'

At Katie's house, Ellen described finding her dolphin waterfall.

'I couldn't believe my eyes' she said. 'When Gail came to see me, I showed her the waterfall, so she went outside and released the dolphins into the ocean. I saw them move and realized they were alive.'

'I know what you mean', said Katie. 'It happened to me too, so I released the dolphins I had as well. Gail and I knew they weren't totally unhappy, but I'm sure you'll agree that they will be a lot happier being free.'

'Yes of course' said Ellen.

'You had a bad dream last night, didn't you Gail?'

'Yes Katie.'

'I could hear you talking through my mind and I saw visions of what you were dreaming' said Katie. 'I know the dreams can be quite scary, but that's what the devil is trying to do. He wants to frighten you and will keep trying until you give in. But I know you won't give in to them Gail. What he is trying to do is weaken your strength by coming into your dreams. He obviously thinks he has a good chance of succeeding and I know that's why White Angel made your powers stronger. 'So don't be afraid to sleep, because if you were they would be winning already. You've got to sleep. Try and go to bed a little earlier tonight.'

'OK Katie', said Gail.

'Just remember that I'm with you in your thoughts and in your dreams so that I can help you and support you.'

'I would be grateful for that.'

'That's what friends are for' said Katie. 'Now I think I'll make us some soup.'

'That would be great Katie, I'm quite hungry.'

Dylan followed Katie into the kitchen.

'Do you want some dinner Dylan?'

He barked, so she gave him and Blacky and little Lucky some dinner. Lucky could obviously smell the food from the living room because she went through to the kitchen and over to where her dinner was.

When they all finished eating their soup, Katie turned to Gail and said: 'I was just thinking Gail, why don't you try your powers?'

'Where, though?' said Gail. 'I don't want to harm anything here.'

'Don't worry, I have an idea' said Katie. 'I'll wish for a massive cave and you can use your powers in there. What do you think? Does that sound like a good idea?'

'Great idea, Katie' said Gail.

So they went outside the cottage, took a right and walked a couple of miles until Katie stopped them.

'This is the perfect spot' she said. 'It's just grass. We can put the cave here. Is that OK with you Gail?'

'Yes, this is fine Katie.'

'Right let's close our eyes and concentrate very hard', said Katie. So they all did so for about five minutes.

'Now open your eyes' said Katie.

They opened their eyes and there it was - a massive cave.

'Right, let's go inside' said Katie. They went inside to see that the cave was all lit up for them so they could see where they were going. As they reached the bottom of the cave, Gail turned to Ellen and said: 'Mum, will you keep Dylan and Blacky beside you, and could you hold Lucky for me too?'

'Of course Gail.'

So Ellen put a leash on Dylan and Blacky so that they would stay beside her, then she held Lucky tight.

'Gail, point your right forefinger out' said Katie. So she did so.

'Now look at the big grey boulder over there. I want you to use your mind and your powers to break it in half. Remember, you really need to concentrate. '

Amazing colours began to come from Gail's finger and on to the boulder. Katie could see the concentration on her face. Then suddenly, with a great cracking noise, the boulder broke in half.

'Oh my god' said Ellen.

Gail opened her eyes.

'That was very good Gail', said Katie. 'Now this may sound silly, but I'm going to wish for a car.'

So Katie closed her eyes and wished for a car. Seconds later, when she opened her eyes, there was a blue BMW right in front of her.

'Right Gail' said Katie. 'Do what you did the last time, OK?'

Gail pointed her right forefinger at the car and started to use her mind and concentrate as before. Once again there were spectacular colours coming from her finger and sparks flying all round her. Abruptly the car blew into little pieces. Gail then opened her eyes.

'That was amazing Gail' said Katie. 'Well done. You have very strong powers. White Angel would be proud of you. She's probably watching you right now in her mind. That was only twice, you have already broken a boulder in half and blown a car to pieces. You should be proud of yourself. You picked it up right away!'

Katie gave her a hug and they went over to where Ellen was standing. Dylan was all over Gail, making a fuss of her. Ellen gave her a cuddle and said 'You've done very well Gail.'

Suddenly Gail heard White Angel's voice.

'Congratulations Gail. You've done very well. Especially for your first time. I knew you were the right person to fight for this world.'

'Thank you White Angel' said Gail.

'Now rest your mind for a while. It keeps the powers strong.'

'OK.'

'I'll be seeing you soon Gail.'

'OK, bye White Angel.'

As they stepped out of the cave Katie wished it gone and it simply vanished, as if it had never been there.

They went back to Katie's for a while. Katie went into the

kitchen and made some coffee and brought it out to them.

'Here you are Gail. I think you could be doing with some caffeine.'

'Yes you're probably right Katie', said Gail.

'Well Gail, we know one thing' said Katie. 'You don't need any more of my help. You seem to know what you're doing.'

'I would prefer it if you were there with me when I'm blowing things up or whatever. Even if it's just for a couple of days until I get used to it. Is that OK with you Katie?'

'Of course Gail', said Katie. 'I'll be there whenever you need me.

When they had drunk their coffee, Katie suggested a game of Monopoly. So they laughed and joked for a while and played a few games. Then Ellen said: 'Look at the time, it's getting late. It's half past ten. We should be going.'

As they went to walk out of the door, Gail turned around to Katie. 'Thank you for everything you've done tonight', she said.

'I appreciate it Katie.'

'I know you do Gail. I'll see you both tomorrow. Goodnight.'

'Good night Katie', said Gail.

So Ellen and Gail made their way home.

As Gail was climbing the stairs that night, she heard a sudden noise. Dylan started barking.

'What is it Dylan?' said Gail.

He went to the door and started to growl, showing his teeth fiercely.

'Dylan was never like that' Gail thought to herself. 'Come here Dylan!' But he wouldn't move. She knew now that something was really wrong. Someone must be outside, and it definitely wasn't her mother or Katie.

She put Dylan and Lucky into the kitchen and put a see-through shield around them to protect them. She was scared in case they got hurt.

'Just my luck' she said to herself. 'I've only just started to use my new powers and I think the devil and the demons obviously know this. I think they want to destroy me before I get really good at using them.'

Very slowly she opened the door, concentrating with her mind and keeping her eyes opened. She heard a voice.

'You know why we are here, don't you Gail?'

'Is it to kill me?'

'No, not yet. We want to take you with us to show
you our world. Haven't you sensed that, Gail?'

'Let's just say you took me by surprise' said Gail. 'The way I see it is, you
must be scared since you decided to come and see me tonight knowing that I
have started using my new powers. I know you will try and get me to go and
live in your world, because you want my powers, and you know that if I don't
go with you, my powers will get stronger and I will be ready to fight you.'

'We have the power' said the demon. 'We just want more, and
that more is you Gail. Believe me, you will give in to us.'

'I will never give in' said Gail. 'I can imagine what your world is full of. At the
end of the day, we should be taking over your world and making it a better place.'

The demon got closer. He was floating in the air. Gail couldn't
see his face. It was just blackness looking back at her.

Then one of his hands came towards her. It was grey and wrinkly all over
and had three long fingers with very long black nails. As he went to grab Gail's
neck, Gail put her left hand out, grabbed the wrinkly hand and swung him
round and round. Then she let him go. She quickly pointed her right forefinger
at him. 'I'm sending you straight back to the evil you came from!' she shouted

Just then a beam of white light shot out from Gail's finger and surrounded the
demon. It flung the demon backwards so fast that he disappeared back into the
world he had come from. As he vanished she heard his voice calling faintly to her.

'We will win!' he shrieked. 'There will be no more chances for you Gail. You
will die!'

Gail leaned against the door for a few minutes. She was
shaking all over. As she looked up at the sky, she thought to
herself: 'Well, at least the demon is gone for now.'

She closed the door and went through to the kitchen, using her mind to take
the see-through shield off Dylan and Lucky. Dylan jumped up on her and licked
her face. Gail hugged him and said: 'It's OK Dylan, it's OK now.' She lifted
Lucky and gave her a little hug too. Then she put the kettle on to have a cup

of lemon tea and sat down at the kitchen table. Her hands were still shaking.

Dylan went over to her and sat beside her and gave her a paw. She stroked his head and cuddled him.

Gail put some whisky in her tea; she knew it would help her relax. Suddenly she could hear White Angel in her mind calling out to her.

'Are you OK Gail?'

'Yes, I'm fine White Angel. I'm just a little shaky.'

'I'm sorry I couldn't get through to you sooner Gail, but for some reason it took me a while' said White Angel. 'You've probably blocked me out by mistake. I felt something was wrong and when I finally got through, I was shown in my mind what had happened. Do you want me to come to you?'

'No White Angel', said Gail. 'It's all right.'

'Considering you've only just become a witch, you handled yourself really well with that demon' said White Angel. 'And you were right, the demon did come to you because he knew you had just been given these powers and wanted to take them from you, or even try and take you back with him. But you showed him, didn't you?'

'Yes, I guess I did' said Gail.

'I'll come and see you tomorrow, OK?'

'You don't have to' said Gail.

'Well, I'm going to' said White Angel. 'The spirit world knows something's going to happen very soon. They'll be watching out for us now and if they want to, they can show themselves. It will even make them stronger to fight because, though their minds are strong, by using their bodies too they will have more power. They have powers similar to ours. Right now outside your cottage, you'll be surrounded by ghosts. You just won't see them yet. So now you can rest easy Gail. Try and get some sleep. I am going to programme happy dreams into your mind to give you a break. OK?'

'OK White Angel', said Gail. 'That would be great.'

'Right, you know what to do Gail. Close your eyes and concentrate very hard.'

Gail closed her eyes and started concentrating and White Angel put her hands on Gail's head and pressed hard. A few minutes later she asked her to open her eyes.

'Right Gail, that's you done' she said. 'I'm going now, but I'll see you tomorrow.'

'OK White Angel, see you tomorrow' said Gail. She lifted Lucky up and called Dylan to come. 'Let's go to bed. I think this time we will get there.' She put little Lucky into her bed and Dylan lay next to Gail on her bed. They all fell asleep right away.

It was not until after ten in the morning that Gail woke up and let out a big yawn. Dylan awoke and jumped off the bed. Little Lucky was still sleeping. She always slept that bit longer.

Gail and Dylan went down the stairs and went through to the kitchen. Gail put the kettle on and then gave Dylan some cornflakes. She then made her lemon tea and went out into the back garden and sat down on the bench. The sun was splitting the sky and it was just the right temperature.

After Gail had taken a shower and got dressed, there was a knock on the door. It was her mum and Katie. She sat them down and started to tell them what had happened the previous evening.

'I know, I heard from White Angel last night' said Katie. 'I'm so sorry I wasn't there for you again. I just don't know what's going on. I think maybe we've got a blockage somewhere. It seems that way because we should always know when something's wrong and be able to pick it up. Anyway, apparently you handled yourself very well.'

'I did OK' said Gail. 'I sent the demon back to where he came from and believe me even though I've these powers, I don't know how I still managed to do what I did.'

'At least you're OK Gail', said Katie. 'That's the main thing.'

'I'm just wondering how strong the powers from the dark side are going to be' said Gail.

'They will be strong, but because we have goodness in us, it makes us more and more strong' said Katie.

'Perhaps we should stay together, especially at night, and take turns in each other's cottages' said Katie. 'What do you think Gail?'

'Well, we don't have to', said Gail. 'We have spirits watching over us now.'

'I know Gail, but I still think we would be safer if we stayed together. Especially for you Gail, because it's you they will come and see.'

'You don't have to worry about me Katie.'

'I know Gail, but I do, and so does your mum. We could help you protect Dylan and Lucky.'

'I can look after them and keep them safe', said Gail. 'I even put a see-through shield around them and they were fine. Do you know, part of it was quite funny.'

'What do you mean?'

'Well, when I went to use my powers to make the see-through shield disappear, I could see Dylan barking but I couldn't hear him. You know I would never let anything happen to Dylan or Lucky, or the other animals. I would die first. You do know that, don't you Katie?'

'Of course I do Gail' said Katie. 'But please will you at least think about all of us staying together at night?'

'OK, I'll think about it', said Gail.

'That's all I ask.'

'White Angel is coming to see us today' said Gail. 'I'm not sure when, but I have a feeling it will be soon. She will call to me first. That's what she usually does. We will need to talk about the blockage that we keep having through our minds. It's strange that it keeps happening. We will need to get it sorted.'

'I agree', said Katie.

'When is it going to happen to me?' said Ellen.

'What do you mean Mum?' asked Gail.

'Well, I thought I would've had some powers by now and if I had them, I could do more to help the both of you.'

'You're absolutely right Mum' said Gail. 'We will definitely sort something out.'

Gail then heard White Angel's voice. 'I'm just on my way to see you Gail' she said.

'OK' said Gail through her mind. 'See you soon.'

'What is it Gail?' said Katie.

'It's White Angel. 5he's coming right now to see us.'

A few seconds later there was a knock on the door, and there was

White Angel. She came into the sitting room and looked at Ellen.

'So Ellen, I hear you would like to have some powers' she said.

'Yes I would love to have powers so that I could help Gail and Katie if they ever needed me.'

'OK, I shall give you the powers' said White Angel. 'Now I want you to stand up.'

Ellen stood up and White Angel put her hands on Ellen's head.

'It's OK Ellen. Don't look so worried. Close your eyes. Now I want you to think about something good that has happened in your life, and through your mind I want you to try and relive it.'

A few minutes later White Angel pressed her hands a little bit harder onto Ellen's head and white sparks started flying out of Ellen's head, just as Gail had experienced. It lasted a few minutes.

'Now Ellen, open your eyes. How do you feel?'

'I'm OK. I just feel a bit strange, that's all.'

'Don't worry, that will pass. Right Katie, you're next. I know you have already got powers, but I'm going to make them stronger. OK?'

'OK' said Katie.

'Now you know what to do' said White Angel.

So Katie closed her eyes tightly and then White Angel put her hands on her head and within seconds blue sparks appeared. As Gail watched, it looked as though Katie was in a deep sleep. Gail knew that the same thing had been done to her. She thought it looked quite scary, though it didn't hurt at all.

White Angel took her hands away from Katie's head. 'Right Katie', she said. 'That's you done. You can open your eyes now. How are you feeling?'

'I feel really good' said Katie. 'I also feel as if I have more energy.'

'That's good, because you will need it' said White Angel. 'I'm going to try something with all of you now. First of all, I want you to close your eyes.'

So they closed their eyes.

'Now then. I want you all to concentrate on what I'm visualizing.'

A few minutes later their eyelids started moving as if they were dreaming, but they were actually visualizing the same thing. When they finally all opened their eyes, White Angel spoke.

'I need to know if you all could see what I was seeing' she said. 'Gail, I would like you to go first.'

'You were watching the seals' said Gail.

'You're absolutely right' said White Angel. 'What about you Ellen? What did you see?'

'I saw you watching the seals too' said Ellen.

'And you Katie? What did you see?'

'I saw you standing next to the water, watching the seals.'

'Well now that our minds are sorted, we shouldn't have any more problems' said White Angel. 'At least you all know that if we ever have problems like this in the future, you know it can be fixed. There shouldn't be any more blockages, but if there are, we will know who's causing them. It will be the devil himself or the demons who will try and block our minds.

'Now Ellen, I want to see you using your powers. I'd like you to wish for anything you want, but you need to concentrate very hard.'

So Ellen began to concentrate really hard and then she made her wish. Suddenly a white vase with red roses in it appeared high in the air.

'Now Ellen, use your mind to lower it down into the palms of your hands.'

So Ellen put her hands out and sure enough the vase landed in her hands. 'Well done Ellen', said White Angel. 'Do you feel slightly drained?'

'Just a little' said Ellen.

It's always like that at the start, but you'll find you'll get the hang of it' said White Angel.

'I'm sure I will', said Ellen. 'I must say, that was some experience. It was very exciting.'

'It's so nice to hear you say that' said White Angel. 'Well, it's time for me to go now Gail, and I hope the three of you will stay together tonight and every other night for that matter. It's the best thing for you to do. I'll be keeping a close eye on all of you tonight in case a demon or demons come back. If that's the case, I'll use my wings for speed and I'll come straight to you. OK Gail?'

'OK', said Gail.

White Angel opened the front door with her mind and as
she stepped outside her feet lifted from the ground.

'Take care of yourself Gail, I'll see you soon' she said, and away she
went flying towards the sky. Gail watched until she couldn't see her any
more. She then closed the door and went through to the living room.

'I need something to eat', said Gail. 'A sandwich or a plate
of soup. Would both of you like something to eat?'

'I would like some toast', said Ellen.

'What about you Katie?' Gail asked. 'What would you like to eat?'

'The same as your mum if that's OK?'

'Of course it is', said Gail. 'It's a very special day for you Mum.'

'Yes it is Gail' said Ellen. 'I can't believe I have powers now. I
made a wish earlier on and I'm just wondering if it came true.'

'What did you wish for?'

'I wished for a big chocolate cake to appear in the fridge'
said Ellen. Gail opened the fridge door to see the chocolate cake.
She started to laugh when she took it out the fridge.

'I don't believe it Mum. Look at the size of it. I'm struggling to try to hold it.'

Ellen got up from the chair and gave Gail a hand to put the
cake on the table. The three of them started laughing and then
Ellen said: 'I really didn't think the cake would be this big.'

When they had stopped laughing, Gail cut some of the cake and
they all enjoyed it. Then they went into the living room to relax.

A couple of hours later they all decided to go for a walk with the
animals. As they reached the ocean, Gail kept her sandals on and
went a little further into the water. She could see the coral.

'Look at all the different colours, Mum' she said.

'I'm looking Gail. It's wonderful.'

All of a sudden Gail saw Dylan's ball flying in the
air. It landed next to Dylan's front legs.

'That ball was in the back garden' said Gail.

'I take it you wished for the ball so Dylan could play with it?' asked Ellen.

'No, Mum' said Gail. 'I didn't wish for that to happen.'

'Maybe it was Katie who made the wish' said Ellen.

'I don't think it was Katie Mum' said Gail. 'I'll ask her anyway when she comes back.'

Ellen held Lucky while Gail threw Dylan's ball for him. A few minutes later Katie came back with Blacky, who went straight over to Dylan wanting to play.

'Blacky seems to have grown already Katie' said Ellen.

'I know', said Katie. 'I can see the difference myself.'

'Listen Katie' said Gail. 'Was it you who made Dylan's ball move from my back garden over to here?'

'No Gail' said Katie. 'It wasn't me.'

'I didn't think it was you Katie' said Gail. 'I just had to ask.'

They all sat down on the golden sand. That's just what it was like - a giant piece of gold which glistened more at night. A while later Gail tried to coax Dylan to go into the water by himself, but he wouldn't. He just stood there looking at Gail with his big brown eyes as if to say: 'Please don't make me go into the water.'

Gail thought that it would perhaps be a good idea to help him with a spell, giving him the courage to go into the water, and then maybe when he was more confident, she could lift the spell gradually from him. She could tell that sometimes when the other dogs were in the water, he wanted to go in with them. Gail just wanted Dylan to enjoy himself like all the other dogs. So she decided to do it.

She closed her eyes and concentrated very, very hard. Then she wished that he wouldn't be afraid any more, and that he could go into the water by himself. She made the spell strong, so it would last a while. When she opened her eyes, she could see Dylan in the water swimming and loving it. She was so happy for him.

She looked over to see where her mum and Katie were. They were a few yards away from her paddling in the water. She could hear them laughing.

When Gail called to Dylan to come out of the water, he came out all wet and started shaking the water off himself. Most of it went over Gail.

'Dylan, are you getting me all wet for the fun of it?' said Gail.

He barked three times as if to say that he was.

'You're a cheeky boy, aren't you?' said Gail and he barked again. Then they went over to join Ellen and Katie and of course little Blacky.

'I see you two are having fun' said Gail.

'Yes, we've been enjoying ourselves' said Katie. 'We nearly fell over, but we managed to hold ourselves up. You would think we had been drinking.'

They started laughing again. It was good to see them having a good time. Blacky was right beside Katie, doing some paddling as well. A while later they came out of the water and sat down on the golden sand. Gail could see the sand glittering on Blacky's coat. It looked amazing next to the black. She reflected that you would never see anything like it back in the world she had left.

'Right, we'd better go back to the cottage' she said aloud. 'It's getting late. First though, I'm going to check on the dogs and the cats.'

'Don't be long' said Katie. 'Listen, why don't we all stay at my cottage tonight?'

'Are you sure?' asked Gail.

'Yes, of course', Katie said. 'It would be great to have you stay over, and of course Dylan and Lucky too.'

'We could even have a couple of drinks' said Ellen.

'Yes sure, but only a couple mind' said Katie. 'I don't want you getting drunk.' They all started laughing.

'Mum, would you take Lucky for me? I think she's tired' said Gail.

'Sure Gail' said Ellen.

'Right. I'm away to check on the dogs. I'll see the both of you soon.'

Ellen and Katie made their way back to the cottage. As Gail was walking towards the dogs' house, she moved her hand over her eyes to check on all the wild animals. They were all doing fine. She put an invisible shield all around them. If she were to touch it from her side, it would electrocute her, so she would remove it with her mind. From the inside, however, it was harmless, so it wouldn't hurt the animals.

As she reached the dogs' house she could hear them barking. It was as if they sensed she was there. She opened the door and said hello to the dogs and they all started going mad, licking her and jumping up. She made a lot of them and gave them all some dinner and a drink of water.

When Gail wasn't actually there in person, she could always be there in her mind. She put a spell on the dogs when they first arrived so that they wouldn't be frightened if they saw anything move. Now they were used to seeing it all the time, and she could talk to them through her mind, so they could hear her. This would settle the dogs down.

She sat for a while with them to give them some company. Later on, she went and opened the back door for them and put the light on above the back door. Then she and Dylan went out into the back garden to join them. Most of the dogs were running about playing with each other. The garden was so big. It was good that all the dogs got on well together. They all had their different personalities, just like humans. All their natures seemed to click, and they would never fight with each other, thankfully. Maybe it was because they were happy and knew they were free now.

A couple of hours later Gail called out to the dogs and they all ran straight inside. She gave them biscuits. She and Dylan then left the house and went to see the cats. It wasn't that far from the dogs' house. When she reached it, a few of the cats went up to her. She opened the front door and went inside to find the other cats lying sleeping on their quilted beds.

Gail went into the kitchen and put some more food out for them with some milk. She suddenly heard meowing, and about twenty of them came into the kitchen. One of the cats rubbed against Gail's leg and was purring loudly. Gail picked him up and said: 'What is it, do you want a cuddle?' She kissed his little face and cuddled him gently.

'There you are', she said. When she put him down he went over to his bowl and ate some food.

Gail gave the house a clean and afterwards she spent some time with the cats and the little kittens. A good while later, she looked at the time. It was ten past ten.

'I think it's time for us to go now Dylan' she said.

She put some treats out for the cats and the kittens and then she and Dylan left the house and made their way back to Katie's. She was looking at the bright stars in the sky when she heard White Angel call to her.

'Gail, can you hear me?'

'Yes' Gail said. 'What's wrong?'

'The war is about to start. It won't be tomorrow, but the next day, so be prepared Gail. I'll be joining you very soon, so get more practice in. OK?'

'OK White Angel.'

Gail had reached Katie's before she remembered that she had forgotten to put a see-through shield around the animals' houses. She stopped walking. Then she closed her eyes and started to concentrate very hard. By using her mind and her powers, she could see the dogs' house. She then put the see-through shield around it to protect the dogs. Then she did the same for the cats' house. She knew they would be safe now.

As she opened her eyes, the door swung open. She and Dylan went in.

'Do you want a drink Dylan?'

'Woof' said Dylan.

Having given him some water, she greeted her mum and Katie.

'Hi Gail', said Katie. 'How are the dogs and the cats?'

'They're fine' said Gail. 'I always feel guilty when I've got to leave them. I think we should move them closer to us, because they must get lonely even though they have each other. It will be easy enough to do.'

'Gail, did you hear from White Angel?'

'Yes I did Katie' said Gail. 'She told me the war was just about to start.'

'Did she say when?'

'The day after tomorrow' said Gail. Could you hear White Angel talking about it?'

'Yes I could' said Katie.

'That's good, at least we know we can hear each other. We don't want any more problems with a war starting.'

'Would you like a cup of lemon tea?' asked Katie.

'Yes that would be nice' said Gail.

'One cup of lemon tea coming up.'

'Well Mum, all we can do now is use the powers we have and just hope and pray that things will be all right.'

Ellen held Gail's hand. 'It's got to be, hasn't it?' she said.

'Gail, would you like me to read your tea leaves again?' asked Ellen.

'You can't read out of this cup mum' Gail said. 'It's lemon tea.'

'Yes I know Gail, but I could make you an ordinary cup of tea as well. Then we'll be able to see what the tea leaves say. It might even give us a clue to what's going to happen.'

'I'm not so sure I want to know' said Gail.

'That's not like you Gail.'

'I know, but this is different Mum.'

'You can think about it Gail, and if you do decide that you want your tea leaves read, I'll do it for you' said Ellen.

Ellen went through to the kitchen to make the tea and brought Gail's cup through to the living room.

'Now drink up' she said.

'It's such a horrible taste Mum' said Gail. 'Every time I drink it, the taste seems to get worse, but I know I have to do it. There are some things in life you've just got to sacrifice, and this is one of them.' She forced a smile.

As Gail finished drinking her tea, the expression on her face was quite funny because the taste was so bad. She gave her mum the cup.

'I'll be back in a minute' said Ellen. She went through to the kitchen and put the cup upside down on to her hand. Then she hit the bottom of the cup three times to release some of the tea leaves out of it, because there is usually too much in the cup, which can make it hard to make anything out. She then went back into the living room.

'Right Gail. Let's see what your tea leaves say. Well, I can see you. You're going to come face to face with someone from another world, and I know who it is.'

Gail just looked at her mum. 'You do?'

'Yes Gail, I do' Ellen said. 'It's the devil himself. There's such a sharp pain in my heart.'

Gail went over to her.

'You'll be OK Mum. Just try and relax.'

'The pain's getting worse' said Ellen.

Gail concentrated very hard and wished for her mum's pain to go

away. The sweat was pouring from her forehead from concentrating
so much. Gail could finally see relief in her mum's eyes.

'How are you feeling now Mum?'

'I'm OK Gail', Ellen said. 'The pain has lifted.'

'Do you know what I think?' said Gail.

'What's that?' said Katie.

'I reckon the devil, or one of the demons, used their minds to hurt my
mother', said Gail. 'Well that's not on.

'I still want to read your cup' said Ellen.

'I don't think you should Mum' said Gail.

'Gail, we must do this!'

'5he's right Gail' said Katie.

Gail sat down right next to her mum in case anything else happened.

'OK, let's try again', said Ellen. 'I can see White Angel. 'She's coming
towards you and the devil is going to destroy her. I'll tell you one thing -
White Angel is going to put up a very, very strong fight. I can see myself
and Katie and we are surrounded by ghosts, but they are there to
help us and are making sure we are safe. There is one thing you don't
need to worry about and that's Dylan and Lucky. They will be safe,
and all the other animals too, even if this war gets really ugly.

'I also see two words in your cup and they're next to the animals
– 'invisible shield'. I take it you know what that means Gail?'

'Yes Mum, I do', said Gail. 'I put transparent shields
all around the animals to protect them.'

'There is a number here, 300. The initial D is above it' Ellen went on.
'l reckon that's the number of demons you will be up against. And not
to forget the devil's powers. As we know, he wants your power badly, but
he knows he has a real fight on his hands. The spirits will let you know
when he will appear, but you'll probably know yourself anyway. At least
we know the spirits are watching all of us and are going to help us. Well
Gail, I've read everything in your cup.' She handed Gail her cup.

'Thanks Mum' Gail said. 'You know mum, you were right to

tell me what was in my cup. At least I know now what's going to happen.' Gail then went through to the kitchen to wash the cup.

'Katie, do you think Gail will be all right?' said Ellen.

'She'll be fine' said Katie. 'She's a lot stronger than you think.'

'What do you think will happen to the animals if we all die?' asked Ellen.

'We will become part of the spirit world, but we can still look after the animals' Katie said. 'We will be able to show ourselves if we want, so they won't ever be alone. We will always stay close to them. Anyway, it might not come to that.'

Gail then came back into the living room. 'I'm going outside to practise my powers' she said.

'We'll come with you' said Katie.

'You don't have to' said Gail.

'We want to, don't we Ellen?'

'Of course we do' said Ellen. Gail lifted Lucky up. 'Come on Dylan' she said. 'Let's go walkies. Are you taking Blacky, Katie?'

'Yes, I think I will' said Katie. 'I think we should go to the same spot as before and wish for a cave, like last time.'

So they left the cottage. It was surprisingly bright outside because the stars lit up the sky so well. You would have thought it was dawn, yet it was night time.

They finally reached the spot where the cave had been before.

'Right', said Katie. 'We all know the routine.' They closed their eyes and concentrated and made their wish. When they opened their eyes, the cave was even bigger.

'I reckon we should leave the cave here when we are done rather than vanishing it' said Katie.

'I agree' said Gail.

They all went into the cave and walked on until they got to the bottom of it.

'Mum, could you look after Dylan and Lucky for me again?' said Gail. 'I don't want them getting too close when I'm using my powers.'

'Of course I will Gail. I'll take Blacky as well.'

So Katie gave Blacky to Ellen. 'Thank you for looking after Blacky for me.'

'No problem' said Ellen.

'Right Gail', Katie said. 'Are you ready to begin?'

'Yes I am' said Gail.

'OK, now this might sound weird, but I'm going to wish for a human being. The thing is, he won't be real' said Katie. 'He will just be an illusion. I want to see you dispose of it. Think of it as a demon and feel the anger that's in you.'

Katie used her mind to wish for a human being, and the next thing, there he was, tall with blond hair and blue eyes and dressed in a dark blue suit. As they were looking at this man, Katie knew that he wouldn't feel anything. There would be no pain or emotion. Katie was the one who had the power over him. She could wish for him to smile or cry or run or jump. Even though he looked so real to them, at the end of the day, he was just an illusion.

'Right Gail, are you ready?' asked Katie.

'Yes, let's do it' said Gail.

She kept her eyes opened and concentrated hard. Then she pointed her right forefinger at him and a beam of white light came from her finger. It was so powerful that the man's body exploded into smithereens.

'Gail, that was amazing!' said Katie. 'You've done it. You built up the power in your mind to do this and you've succeeded. You should find that destroying the demons shouldn't be too hard.'

'But Katie, who knows what the demons are capable of? Or the devil for that matter? You know as well as I do how powerful he is.'

'I know how powerful he is Gail, but believe me, we've got just as much power as he has' said Katie. 'Do you want to practise more?'

'Do you think I should?'

'Well in my opinion, you don't need to after what you have just done to that human being' said Katie. 'You've got full marks for that.'

'OK then' said Gail. 'Let's go back to the cottage.'

They left the cave and went back to Katie's. She made them tea and toast and then gave Dylan, Blacky and Lucky some dinner.

'It's been a long day', said Katie.

'It certainly has' said Ellen.

'Mum, are you feeling OK?'

'Yes Gail. I'm just a little shocked about what I saw, but I'm fascinated as well.'

'As long as you're OK Mum.'

'Honestly, I'm fine Gail' said Ellen.

'Well, I'm going to bed' said Katie. 'See you both in the morning.'

'OK, goodnight' said Ellen and Gail.

Lucky was lying on Gail's lap and Dylan was on the chair, fast asleep.

'Listen Gail', Ellen said. 'If you can't sleep tonight or even if you have a bad dream, just you come and wake me. OK?'

'OK Mum, I definitely will' said Gail.

'Well I'm going to bed as well' said Ellen. 'Which room shall I use?'

'I think you've to sleep in the room near the bathroom' said Gail.

'OK Gail. Well, goodnight.'

'Goodnight Mum.'

Gail stayed up for a while watching television. Although her eyes were on the TV set, her mind was elsewhere. She felt wetness on her hand, and looked down to see Dylan licking it.

'Hi Dylan' she said. 'I think maybe it's time we went to bed.'

She took Lucky from her lap and held her, then told Dylan to come and get some sleep. She went into the room downstairs. She thought it would be better if she slept downstairs in case an unexpected visitor appeared, like maybe a demon. She lay on the bed and Dylan lay in between her arms. They all soon fell asleep.

As Gail was dreaming, she saw herself standing beside the ocean looking for the dolphins. Everything was so peaceful, and then suddenly something made her turn around and she could see someone approaching her. But that someone was walking for a change. He had long dark hair and was dressed in black. His eyes were deep red, almost the colour of blood. When he moved to put his hand on her face, Gail noticed his long black fingernails.

'What do you want?' said Gail.

'You know what the hell I want' said the man.

'I want you and your precious world.'

'Well you're never going to get me or my world' said
Gail. 'So why don't you just start facing it?'

'There is one thing about me Gail' said the man. 'That is that I never give up.'

'Well maybe you should', said Gail. 'Who are you anyway? Are you the devil?'
Her tone of voice was challenging. 'Or was it the devil who sent you to me?'

'You know Gail, I'm surprised. With your powers you should know who I am.'

'Maybe I do know who you are. Maybe I was just playing with you.'

'OK, if you're that sure who I am, why don't you tell me?' said the man.

'OK, I will tell you' said Gail. 'Your name is Lucifer.'

'You're absolutely right Gail' said the devil in his deep voice. 'When
you were born, you should have been given to me. I could have changed
your life, but whenever I tried to come near you, something would stop
me from getting to you. Even though I had powers, I didn't realize at
the time that it was you who was stopping me. You even smiled at me,
as if you knew what you were doing, even though you were just a child.
Well Gail, I'm smiling now at you and I'll take what's mine.'

'These powers will never belong to you, Lucifer!' said Gail.

'That's where you're wrong Gail' said the devil. 'Those powers will be mine.'

He touched her face again. Gail could feel her skin burning, but she didn't
move. She wouldn't let him see that it hurt. Instead she just smiled at him.

'Do you find pain amusing, Gail?' asked Lucifer.

'No', she said, still smiling at him.

'I know you'll come around eventually Gail. And even if my side loses,
which we won't, you'll be begging to come with me' said Lucifer.

'Never, do you hear me, never!' said Gail. 'You would have to take me dead!'

He walked away, and the darkness surrounded him and took him back
to his dark world. Suddenly the sky turned blue and the ocean too. The
golden sand started to shine again and a little white rabbit came up to Gail.
She bent down and lifted it up and gave it a cuddle and a kiss. She noticed
the rabbit had light blue eyes, which was strange, she thought to herself.

'Where did you come from, little rabbit?' Gail said.

She then went back to her own cottage and passed right through the front door like a ghost. Then she went upstairs to the bedroom. She saw herself lying there on the bed. She went over to where she was, lay on top of herself and sank into her body. She closed her eyes and fell asleep straight away.

A few hours went by and Gail woke up. Strangely enough, she was still holding the rabbit. Dylan was staring at her as if to say: 'Is this another member of the family?'

'Morning Dylan' said Gail, stroking him. She knew Dylan would be even more jealous now, but what could she do? She just couldn't have left the rabbit, and she knew that it must have been fate for the rabbit to have come to her.

She got up and looked at the time - ten past ten in the morning. Little Lucky woke up early for a change, so Gail lifted her up as well, holding her in one arm and the rabbit in the other.

'Come on Dylan', she said. 'Let's go and get some breakfast.'

She went down the stairs and through to the kitchen and put the kettle on. She gave Dylan some cornflakes and Lucky some kitty food. She then gave the rabbit some lettuce. 'I wonder what other surprises are in store for me' she said out loud. She made herself a cup of lemon tea and some toast with marmalade on it. All you could hear in the kitchen was Dylan, Lucky and the rabbit munching away at their food.

When they were all done, Dylan went over to Gail first for a pet. Gail stroked and cuddled him and said: 'You're my boy, aren't you Dylan?'

'Woof woof' said Dylan.

Then Lucky jumped on Gail's lap and was purring away. The rabbit went over and lay next to Gail's feet.

Just then, there was a knock on the door, and Gail called for the visitor to come in. It was Ellen.

'Gail, where have you been?'

'What do you mean, Mum?'

'You were supposed to stay at Katie's last night' said Ellen. 'Don't you remember? When I went to bed, you were still at Katie's sitting in the living room.'

'Wait a minute, I do remember Mum. When I went to bed last night, I had a weird dream. I was standing outside and the devil approached me.'

'The devil?'

'Yes mum, the devil. The two of us had words and then he disappeared back into the darkness. Then all of a sudden a little white rabbit came up to me. So I lifted the rabbit up and for some reason I went back to my own cottage and went upstairs to my bedroom. I saw myself lying on the bed. Dylan was next to me sleeping and little Lucky was in her bed. So I lay on top of my body and just sank right into myself. I was still holding the rabbit and then I fell asleep. I don't even know how Dylan and Lucky got here.'

'This is so weird, Gail' said Ellen.

'Mum, is Katie all right?'

'Yes, she's fine. You know you gave me such a fright this morning when I saw you weren't at Katie's.'

'I'm sorry Mum' said Gail. 'I didn't mean to frighten you.'

'At least I know you're OK now' said Ellen.

'Mum, you don't need to worry about me', said Gail. 'Remember I'm a witch now and I have powers. I can take care of myself.'

'I know Gail, but I still worry about you' said Ellen.

'Come on Mum, I'll make us a cup of tea and then we'd better go to Katie's.'

'I see you've adopted another animal.'

'Yes it looks that way, doesn't it' said Gail. 'I couldn't leave the rabbit on its own.'

'You know something Gail, you're too soft' said Ellen.

'I know Mum, I can't help it. I just love animals and I would do anything for them. After all, they do need us to look after them.'

'You'll end up taking one of the bears home one of these days.'

They both started laughing. When they had finished drinking their tea, Gail went out into the back garden and wished for a massive hut for the rabbit. Within seconds it appeared. The rabbit went into the hut by itself, as if it knew the hut was for him. Gail put some food and water in the hut for him and then they left to go to Katie's. When they arrived, the front door as usual opened by itself. Katie was in the kitchen, making a pot of coffee. They went through and sat down at the table.

'Where were you both?' asked Katie. 'I got up to make you breakfast

114

and then I realized you weren't around. Is everything OK?'

'Yes, everything's fine', said Ellen.

Gail thought it was a little strange that Katie hadn't sensed what had happened. Maybe she had been in a deep sleep; that would explain how she hadn't picked up what Gail was dreaming about. It worried Gail, because if that had been an emergency, Katie wouldn't have known. The lack of communication between them was getting Gail down. She knew something had to be done about it. It was happening too much.

Another thought crossed Gail's mind. Maybe it could have been the devil who had caused the communication problem, and if that was so it was working, which was a worry. Gail opened the back door and asked Katie if she minded her going into the back garden.

'No, of course not' said Katie.

So Gail lifted Lucky up and called Dylan to come along into the garden. She was admiring the flowers. There were white roses and daffodils and white lilies and as Gail was looking at the roses, two more of them blossomed. Gail went over and sat on the bench next to the dolphin waterfall. She closed her eyes and listened to the water running. She found it very relaxing. She was hoping that White Angel would contact her soon. Katie and Ellen went outside to join Gail.

'What are you thinking about Gail?' asked Ellen.

'Oh nothing, I'm just relaxing, that's all', said Gail.

'I know what you are thinking about' said Katie.

'You do?'

'Yes, of course', said Katie. 'You're wishing that White Angel would come and see you, aren't you?'

'Yes I am' said Gail. But she couldn't understand how Katie would know that, since she didn't know what had happened last night. Maybe the devil's power could only block minds for so long and then like a switch it turned itself off.

Just then Gail heard White Angel calling to her.

'Can you hear me Gail?' she was saying.

'Yes, I can hear you' Gail said.

'I'll be coming to get you in an hour. So get ready.'

'OK' said Gail. 'Well. this is it. The war is about to begin.'

They all went back into the cottage and Katie locked the door. She felt quite sad, because she had never had to do that before. She had always felt safe. Gail put her hand over her face. Keeping her eyes open, she checked on all the animals and wildlife and made sure the see-through shields were secure enough to protect them. When she was finished, she turned to Katie.

'Listen Katie' said Gail. 'Would it be OK with you if we use one of the rooms as a protected area for Dylan, Lucky, Blacky and the rabbit?'

'Of course it would' said Katie.

'Right, I'd better go and get the rabbit' said Gail.

'OK, but hurry back.'

When Gail got to the cottage, she went round to the back and opened the hut. 'Come on then little rabbit. Let's get you safe.' But on her way back to Katie's, she suddenly heard an evil laugh. It sounded so close to her that she started walking faster. When she finally got there, the door opened on its own and Gail went in.

'Mum!' she shouted.

Ellen came straight into the hall. 'What is it Gail?'

'Mum, will you take the rabbit?' Gail said. 'I need to go and put a see-through shield round the dolphins as well.'

'Can't you do it with your mind?'

'Yes, I could Mum, but it's not like I've got far to go. It's only outside.'

Down at the ocean, Gail could see no sign of the dolphins. She put her hand across her face and then suddenly they appeared. They were quite a distance away. She started to concentrate very hard, and began to move her right forefinger as if she was drawing with it and made sure the dolphins had plenty of space to move around in. Once again she used her right forefinger to put a transparent shield around them. She could hear them quite loudly, and it was as if they knew what was going on. She brought them a little closer with her mind and smiled at them.

'Don't worry. You'll all be safe, and that's a promise!'

She blew them a kiss and then moved them back with her mind to where they had been.

On returning to Katie's, she locked the front door.

'Right', she called out. 'That's all the animals safe
and even if we don't make it, they will.'

Dylan was making whimpering noises and his eyes were full of water. He
went over to Gail, licked her hand and looked at her with his big brown eyes.

'You know what's going on, don't you Dylan?' said Gail.

He barked as if to say yes.

'Everything will be OK' she said, and burst into tears. Dylan
meant the world to her. She loved him so much and knew she
had to win, for him and for Lucky and the rabbit too.

'Mum I want you to stay with Dylan, Lucky and
the rabbit. Could you do that for me?'

'But Gail, I want to come with you so that I can help you fight' said Ellen.

'Listen mum, you would be helping me a lot more if you do this for
me' said Gail. 'I'll be putting a shield around you and the animals so that
nothing will happen to you. You will all be safe. At least when I leave here,
I will know that my animals, especially Dylan, won't be so alone.'

'OK Gail, I'll look after them', said Ellen.

'Thank you mum. I appreciate it.'

'Gail, what about the other animals?' said Ellen.

'Yes, I know Mum. I'll put a spell on them, so they won't be afraid.'

She used her mind and put her hand in front of her face to see the
seals and put a spell on all of them, and then the bears appeared and she
put a spell on them too. After the bears, she saw the elephants and she put
a spell on them as well, and then all the other animals, including the dogs
and cats, so if they heard anything loud, they wouldn't be frightened.

'Well at least I know the animals won't be scared now' she thought.

All they needed to do now was wait for White Angel. They all sat down
at the kitchen table and Katie made some sandwiches for them and some
tea, and then she gave all the animals their dinner. Dylan finished his dinner
quickly and then went over and sat down right beside Gail. She gave Dylan
a kiss and a cuddle. Her eyes were full of tears. She was looking at Dylan's
eyes and wondering to herself if this was the last time she would be able to

see his face, because there might not be a tomorrow for her, only him.

'You're a special boy, aren't you Dylan?' said Gail.

His tail was wagging and he kept licking her face as if to tell her that he loved her. She hugged him tight and said that she loved him too.

'I'm going to do my best to win' said Gail.

There was a knock on the door.

'It's White Angel Katie. Would you go and open the door?'

As Katie let White Angel in she noticed that outside there were quite a few other figures and they seemed to be transparent. They must be spirits.

'Katie, where are you?' shouted Ellen.

'I'm just coming' she said. She closed the door and locked it and then went into the living room to join them.

'Do you know what I just saw outside my door?' said Katie. 'Ghosts.'

'That's right Katie' said White Angel. 'Remember I told you they would be here to help us.'

'Oh wait a minute, I do remember' said Katie. 'I don't know why but for some reason I forgot. I'm sorry White Angel.'

'Don't apologize' said White Angel. 'There's been so much going on in our minds lately. I'm not surprised you forgot. The main thing is they're here for us now. Gail, you and I should stay close. That way we can make our power stronger.'

'OK' said Gail.

'Ellen, you are doing the right thing by looking after the animals, because at the end of this you may be the only human survivor, and it will be up to you to keep things going' said White Angel. 'I know it's a lot of responsibility, but that's the way it might go. Don't look so worried Ellen.'

'Can you blame me?'

'Listen, I have to think this way just in case, but I want you to know that I feel very positive that our side will win' said White Angel.

'I hope you do. I will pray for all of you' said Ellen.

'Thank you Ellen' said White Angel. 'I'm sure that will help. How are you holding up, Gail?'

'I'm fine, but Dylan won't leave my side.'

'I can see that. He obviously loves you and believe me, he knows what's going on.'

'Yes, I know that'.

They all sat waiting for a signal from the spirits. Minutes later Gail got up from the chair and started pacing up and down the room. She was shaking a little and her face had turned pale.

'Gail, are you feeling OK?' said Ellen.

'Yes, Mum, I'm OK.'

'Why have you turned pale all of a sudden?'

'It's probably because I'm a little worried and stressed' said Gail. 'But honestly mum, I'll be fine. I'm sure it will pass.'

White Angel went over to Gail and said: 'Are you OK Gail?'

'Yes, I'm fine' said Gail. 'I'm just feeling a little stressed. Can you please tell my mum I will be fine. She worries too much.'

'Well Gail, you do look quite pale and your mum has every right to be concerned' said White Angel. 'Now then, I'm going to try and make you feel better.'

She put her hands onto Gail's head and then closed her eyes. A few minutes later White Angel opened her eyes and took her hands away from Gail's head.

'How do you feel now Gail?'

'I feel so much better. Thank you White Angel.'

'You're welcome.'

Katie was sitting on the carpet playing with Blacky and little Lucky, and Ellen sat right next to Gail holding the rabbit. White Angel was sitting on the sofa with eyes closed and was concentrating. Suddenly a white glow came from her clasped hands. She opened her eyes and one of the spirits spoke to her through her mind.

'It is time', the spirit said.

White Angel stood up and looked at Gail. She had heard the spirit too. She got up from the sofa and looked straight back at White Angel.

'This is it, I guess', said Gail.

'Yes it is', said White Angel.

'Right mum. It's time for you to go into the protected room, and all the animals too.' Ellen started to cry.

'Please Mum, don't cry' said Gail.

'Gail, stay safe' said Ellen.

'I will Mum' said Gail. 'Don't worry. Come on Dylan.'

She lifted up Lucky and the rabbit and took them to the room. She gave them a kiss and a cuddle.

'When I get back I'll think of a name for you. OK little rabbit?' She put both of them down on to the floor. Then she went over to Dylan and looked into his eyes.

'I'm going to miss you Dylan. If I don't make it, I'll be here in spirit to look after you, and at least you will have Ellen to take care of you' said Gail. 'I love you Dylan.' She hugged him for a few minutes and then gave him a kiss.

'Take good care of them for me Mum' said Gail.

'I will Gail.'

'And Mum, no matter what happens, you can rest assured that you will be fine' said Gail. 'Now there is plenty of food for you and the animals.

'Gail, will I be able to still wish for things if I run out?'

'Of course Mum. I just wanted to make sure you had enough of everything before I leave. Listen Mum, I've decided that rather than using only one room to protect you, I'll put a shield all around the cottage. At least that way you'll have plenty of room to move about.'

So Gail concentrated very hard, then she pointed her right forefinger out and moved it towards each and every room, putting a see-through shield around each. When she was finished, she turned to Ellen.

'Right Mum, all the rooms are done, including the hallway', said Gail. 'I'm going to have to go now.' Ellen gave her a hug and a kiss on the cheek.

'See you soon Gail.'

'Yes Mum' said Gail. 'See you soon.'

White Angel gave Ellen a hug and said: 'Now listen, don't you be worrying, just you look after the animals, OK?'

'I will', said Ellen. 'Please take care of yourself, White Angel.'

'I will' said White Angel. 'Katie, I think maybe you should stay here with Ellen.'

'But I should be out there fighting with you and Gail!'

'I think it would be best if you stayed here and looked after Blacky. And another thing. If anything should go wrong, you'll know what to do, and I really wouldn't want Ellen to be alone. Can you understand why I want you to do this? Can you try to, please? I don't want you to think I'm leaving you out, because I'm not, OK?'

'OK', said Katie. 'It's probably for the best that I stay here anyway. I wouldn't want to see Ellen left her on her own, knowing she would have to deal with everything.'

'I'm so glad you're doing this' said White Angel. 'It makes me feel a lot better knowing you'll be here with Ellen to keep an eye on things. And I'm sure Ellen will feel more secure knowing that you're here. At least you wouldn't be leaving Blacky behind.'

'I know', said Katie. 'I'm grateful for that.'

White Angel gave Katie a hug and said: 'Take care of yourself.'

'You take care too, White Angel.'

'Wait a minute' said Gail. 'I forgot to do the outside of the cottage.'

As they went out Gail concentrated again. By moving her forefinger she put a transparent shield around the cottage.

'Right, that's me finished. We can go now. Mum, remember to lock the door.'

'OK Gail' said Ellen.

'Katie, are you coming?' said Gail.

'No, I'm staying here to help keep an eye on things' said Katie.

'OK then see you both soon', said Gail.

'Gail, take my hand', said White Angel.

Gail took White Angel's hand and their feet started to lift from the ground as they began to fly upwards. Gail could hear Dylan whimpering even from where she was. Tears were running down her face. Could this really be the end?

As they flew, Gail could feel the wind against her face. It seemed so powerful.

'Hold on tight Gail' said White Angel. 'It won't be long until we are there.'

Eventually they came to a black sky.

'Where are we going?' said Gail.

'We are just about there' White Angel replied.

A blue glow appeared and White Angel said: 'Gail, we are going towards that blue glow.' As they got closer to it, Gail could see a lot of movement in the dark sky, but she couldn't make out what it was.

'Right Gail, it's time to land' said White Angel.

'Where, though?' asked Gail. 'It's all just blackness. I can't really see anything.'

'Trust me' said White Angel.

Suddenly Gail could see her reflection. 'Look White Angel, is that water I can see, because I can see my reflection?' she asked.

'Yes it is, and that's where we are going to land.'

When they landed on the water, for some strange reason their feet didn't get wet. 'This is amazing!' said Gail. 'I can't believe my feet are still dry.'

'It's amazing what the power of the mind can do' said White Angel.

'Why did we land on water, and why is it so black?'

'The water is a protection', said White Angel.

'What do you mean?'

White Angel spoke quietly and said: 'Well Gail, I do know that the demons won't go into water and that's because a long time ago apparently a lot of them died in it. There was no explanation. I reckon this black ocean is alive, and for some strange reason it won't destroy us. I think maybe this was once a special place too. Who knows? Gail, can you see a red glow in the distance?'

'Yes, I see it' said Gail.

'That's where the demons are. They won't fight near the water or even go in it for that matter. They will only fight when they're high in the air.'

'That's strange.'

'I know' said White Angel. 'Gail, remember when you saw some movement in the sky?'

'Yes, I remember.'

'Do you know who they are?'

'I'm not sure.'

'Try and think who it could be' said White Angel.

So Gail closed her eyes tightly and concentrated and all of a sudden she could hear different voices talking among themselves. When she finally opened her eyes, she said: 'I do know who they are. It's the spirits who have come to help us.'

'That's right Gail. They followed us from our home.'

Just then White Angel noticed that the red glow had turned to an orange colour.

'Right Gail' said White Angel. 'Let's go towards the sky. The demons are coming for us. They are ready to fight.'

They removed their feet from the water and started flying towards the sky. Gail had special wings now, just like White Angel's. As they reached the sky, they could see the demons coming towards them. They were wearing black hooded cloaks and their faces were all wrinkly and grey. They all had big sharp pointed teeth and glowing red eyes. Their hands were also wrinkly and grey, but they weren't ordinary hands. They had three very long fingers with nails that were black. There were so many of them.

Suddenly there was a loud bang and then the whole place started to shake heavily as if it was about to explode. Then there was a loud roaring noise and where the orange glow was shining, something was moving. It was like a black shadow and seemed to get bigger and bigger. Suddenly it started moving fast, straight into the sky. The black figure appeared right in front of Gail, and then it transformed into the beast himself.

White Angel pushed right in front of Gail and said: 'Lucifer, your fight is with me, not Gail.'

He went to hit White Angel, but she grabbed him by his throat and said: 'You're not so tough now, are you Lucifer?'

With his deep voice he said: 'I'll show you what's tough, bitch!'

He lifted her up and his eyes looked like they were on fire. They were burning red. He then threw her, but just as she was about to fall into the water below, her wings opened up and she flew right back up to the sky. Lucifer had hold of Gail.

'We could stop this war now Gail if you come with me' he said.

'I don't think so', said Gail. She stared right into his eyes and concentrated as hard as she could. Her eyes were also on fire, and they were real flames. It was her new power that had created the flames in her eyes, but the strangest thing was, she couldn't feel the flames. There was no pain.

Lucifer was starting to feel pain all over his body and let out a big roar. Gail was trying to explode the inside of his brain, but she wasn't succeeding. His pain started to go away, for Gail was beginning to lose some of her power. White Angel quickly took Gail's hand and used her own mind to help give Gail more power. Suddenly, Lucifer's eyes turned black and his face became a deep red blood-like colour. Huge black horns appeared on his head. He grabbed hold of them with his red hands and as they were trying to get away, he set the both of them on fire with his mind. But even though White Angel and Gail were covered in flames, Lucifer could see their faces and they were smirking at him. He couldn't understand why they weren't screaming or why they weren't in any pain.

All of a sudden the flames disappeared and White Angel said: 'So Lucifer, did you think that that was going to kill us?'

'I knew the flames wouldn't hurt you, witch', said Lucifer. 'I was just testing my powers. I also wanted to see the both of you covered in flames. It sort of makes me feel good.'

He said that to them because he didn't want them thinking that he didn't know about the flames.

'If I really wanted to, I could kill both of you right now, but I think I'll wait and let the demons have a go first' said Lucifer.

'They can try but they will fail' said White Angel.

'That's what you think' said Lucifer. Then he disappeared.

White Angel said: 'Right Gail. Let's get this war over with.'

Gail could hear loud noises. 'Where are those noises coming from White Angel?'

'It's the spirits' said White Angel. 'They are fighting the demons. Use your wings and go a little higher into the sky and you'll be able to see them.'

Gail used her wings to fly further into the sky. 'I can see them and they're fighting with their arms and legs' she said. 'I don't understand. Why aren't the spirits using their minds?'

'They are using their minds Gail, and because they've shown themselves now and have become real again, they have more power', said White Angel. 'Anyway, we should be over there helping them.'

'Let's go then' said Gail.

So White Angel and Gail flew over to where the demons were and went right among them. They both very quickly concentrated and then pointed their right forefingers out and started using their powers. Sparks were flying everywhere. One by one they started to destroy the demons by blowing them into pieces. As the demons were using up their powers, their eyes became red and glowing. They started throwing balls of fire, but White Angel and Gail used their minds to stop the fire from getting too close to them. Then they threw the balls of fire right back at the demons and a couple of them exploded into smithereens.

'Who's next?' said Gail.

A couple of demons approached her and went to grab her. She stopped them by grabbing them with her powerful hands. Then she threw one of the demons into the air and pointed her left forefinger at the demon. A beam of light came from Gail's finger and went straight on to the demon. As she moved her finger round in a circle, the demon suddenly caught fire. Within a couple of seconds his whole body had exploded.

The other demon used his power to hurl a fireball at the back of Gail's head, but just as it was about to hit her White Angel put her hand in front of it and sent it back at the demon Gail was holding. Then she sent the fireball into the demon's head.

'Let go Gail!' she shouted. Gail let the demon go. Seconds later his head exploded and the rest of the body fell into the water below.

'What the hell happened there?' said Gail.

'You were nearly joining the spirit world Gail' said White Angel.

'What do you mean?'

'There was a fireball right at the back of your head' said White Angel. 'I just stopped it in time.'

'Thanks for that' said Gail.

'Are you OK?'

'Yes, I'm fine' said Gail. 'Just think. I could have been going to meet my maker.'

'Well thankfully Gail you're still here, but remember to always look around you' said White Angel.

They blew up a few more demons.

'Stay close to me Gail', said White Angel. 'It makes the power stronger.'

The spirits were now fighting and winning. Even when the demons did kill spirits, it wouldn't matter, because even though they had showed themselves to be real, they were still dead. Many of the demons were falling into the black water after being destroyed by the spirits, and being such a dark place, it was surrounded by colour, as if fireworks were going off.

Suddenly a strange thing happened. Red eyes appeared in the black sky. Fierce eyes - the devil's eyes. The whole place started to shake as if everything was about to blow up.

'Gail, take my hand', said White Angel, and they both flew into the black sky and then went through some grey clouds.

White Angel called out: 'Let's stop here Gail.'

'Why do we have to stop here?' said Gail. 'What is it?'

'The devil is going to blow the whole lot up Gail' said White Angel. 'This is going to be some explosion, unless we do something.'

'There must be something we can do' said Gail.

'Gail' a voice hissed.

'Is that you, Lucifer?'

'You know it's me, Gail', said Lucifer. 'Stop playing around.'

'Tell me something Lucifer' said Gail. 'Why in the hell would you want to blow your own place up?'

'Because I can. I do what I want, but when I do this, it will affect some of your world. You may have protected some of it, but there are some things I can still destroy and believe me, I will do it unless...'

'Unless what?' said Gail.

'Unless you come with me' said Lucifer. 'After all, you do belong to us.'

'I told you before that your fight is with me, not Gail' shouted White Angel. 'And after all, it is my world that you want.'

'No no!' he shouted aggressively. 'I want Gail, and I want her now.'

'Maybe I should go. At least it would put a stop to all of this' said Gail.

'No Gail, you're wrong' said White Angel. 'It wouldn't stop, because after he's taken your powers from you, he will kill you and then destroy our world anyway.'

Suddenly the whole place began to catch fire. White Angel said: 'Right I'm ready for him. Gail I want you to stay here.'

'No, I won't stay', said Gail. 'I want to help you.'

'I'm trying to protect you Gail' said White Angel.

'Well, two of us is better than one' said Gail.

'What about three of us?' someone said, and Gail felt a touch on her shoulder. She slowly turned around, not knowing what to expect, and there in front of her was her grandmother. She looked just the same as Gail remembered her. She had blue eyes and grey hair and was wearing a long deep blue dress and a long black coat which was open. The buttons down the left side of the coat were gold and really shiny.

'Gran, what are you doing here?'

'I'm here to help you Gail, and although I'm a spirit now, I can still help you from my side. As you know we as spirits have some powers too.

'Gran, this is White Angel.'

'Yes I know', said Magdalene. 'We've met.'

'You've met?' said Gail.

'I know all the spirits, but only so many have been chosen to come here to help you' said White Angel.

'Sorry I wasn't here sooner, but it took me some time to get here', said Magdalene. Gail hugged her and told her she had missed her.

'I've missed you too Gail', said Magdalene. 'Now let's get this war over with.'

They all held hands and flew through the grey clouds. By this time the fire was getting out of control. The flames were near enough reaching the sky, and the spirits were still fighting the demons.

'White Angel, Gail, follow me', said Magdalene.

'Shouldn't we be helping the spirits?' said Gail.

'It's OK Gail' said Magdalene. 'The spirits can handle the demons. They have already destroyed quite a lot of them as you know. Now then, let's go.'

So the three of them started to fly through the flames. As they were among them, they could still see the orange glow which was not far from where they were. Eventually when they reached the orange glow, Magdalene called out: 'Right both of you. Down this way.'

The three of them flew downwards until they got to a black

gate, which they noticed was locked. Magdalene went right
through the gate and waited for Gail and White Angel.

'Right Gail' said White Angel. 'Let's concentrate.'

So they both concentrated hard and by using their minds, they broke
the lock. Magdalene then opened the gate for them and Gail closed it
behind her. They went down a flight of black shiny steps, and when they
finally reached the bottom they noticed that the ground was as black and
shiny as the steps. It was like a massive cave, lit up by real fire. As they
walked further into the cave, they could hear screaming and crying.

'Where are the screams coming from?' said Gail.

'They're coming from the bottom of the cave', said Magdalene.

So the three of them started walking faster towards the end of the cave. When
they finally got there, they came across some men and women who were chained
to the cold red walls. Blood was pouring from their arms where the chains were
cutting into them, and they had chains on their ankles and they were bruised all
over. White Angel started to concentrate with her mind. She used her powers
to break all the chains apart, releasing the men and women. Some of them had
fallen to the ground, so Gail and Magdalene went over to help them up. Gail
then quickly wished for some water, clothes and blankets. Though it was quite
hot in the cave, the men and women who had been chained up were shivering.

'They must have been down here for a long
time, maybe years' said White Angel.

The clothes they did have on were like rags. White Angel kept a
look out while Gail and her gran started to bathe some of the men
and women. The cuts were so bad that they were infected.

'Gran, look at this man's arm' said Gail. 'I think it's gangrenous.'

Just then there was a massive roar in the cave.

'It's Lucifer!' said White Angel. 'Quick, let's gather round.'

They all held hands and started to use their minds and their
powers. Sparks were flying everywhere, from all three of them.
Lucifer reached the bottom of the cave and approached them.

'How dare you come into my home! Especially you Gail.'

'I had to see what it looked like' Gail said sarcastically. 'I see you have been doing your usual. Making people suffer.'

'Well that's what I'm here for' said Lucifer. 'After all, I do know that they enjoy the pain.'

While Gail was speaking to him, she was still concentrating with White Angel and Magdalene.

'Well you won't be hurting anyone any more' she said 'You're finished.'

Lucifer let out a roar. 'Now you listen to me bitch! You're the ones that will be finished, not me. Do you hear me?'

Gail just looked at him, but she didn't say anything. As Lucifer went to grab Gail's throat, she used her powers, lifted him from the ground and then threw him against the walls. He fell on the ground. When he had struggled to his feet, he shouted to Gail: 'Is that the best you can do?' and let out an evil laugh.

Gail, White Angel and Magdalene now started talking to each other through their minds. Together they all wished for a massive rocket. All of a sudden a huge rocket appeared right in front of them.

'Do you think that that will kill me?' said the devil.

'I know it will' said Gail.

Suddenly fire appeared all around them in a circle. White Angel called out: 'Let's do it now.'

The three of them wished for the rocket to go straight into Lucifer. It lifted itself off the ground and started moving very slowly towards Lucifer. Lucifer used his powers to make the rocket turn round and go straight back to Gail, but just as it was about to strike her chest, Magdalene pushed Gail out of the way and then White Angel turned the rocket around using her mind. It went straight towards Lucifer. He was about to avoid it, but White Angel took one hand of the rocket and got a hold of one of his horns. Just as the rocket was about to go through him, White Angel let go of it. Lucifer exploded into little pieces with a massive roar.

'Well I didn't expect for this to go so easily' said White Angel. 'Thanks to you Magdalene, we succeeded.'

Gail gave Magdalene a hug and said: 'You're our hero, Gran. I'm just so glad you're here.'

'A part of me will always be here Gail, in case you need me',
said Magdalene. 'I'll be here for your mother too. I will always
be around somewhere looking out for the two of you.'

'Right, let's get these people out of here', said Magdalene. White
Angel and Gail started putting blankets around the men and women.

'Right, let's go' said Gail.

They all started walking through the cave. Some of the women
were struggling. Their ankles and their feet were all swollen.

'It's OK' said Gail. 'You're all going to be fine.'

When they finally got to the black steps, White Angel turned round and said
'I want you all to listen. I'm going to help you. What I'm about to say might seem
strange, but to make things easier, I'm going to make you all fly up these steps.
Just don't be afraid. As you can see we are here to help you, but first I'm going to
check if it's safe outside, because I don't know if all the demons are dead or not.'

White Angel flew up the steps and opened the black gate. She then
flew towards the orange glow. When she reached it, she looked up at
the sky and all around her and saw that everything was calm.

Suddenly someone touched her shoulder from behind. White Angel
turned quickly to see who it was; it was one of the spirits. He had short dark
hair and blue eyes and was wearing a black coat and black trousers.

'I've come to tell you that the demons are all dead' he said. 'It's only us ghosts
that are out here now. We saw you destroy Lucifer through our minds. I and all the
other spirits would like to say that we thought you were brave for what you did.'

'Thank you' said White Angel. 'I've always known spirits could see things in
their minds just like us, but being able to fight demons and using your minds as
well, that's something. I've met most of the spirits, but I don't think I've met you.'

'No, you haven't' said the spirit. 'I only died a month ago.'

'I'm sorry to hear that' said White Angel.

'Don't be' said the spirit. 'I'm happier than I've
ever been. And do you know something.'

'What's that?'

'Even though I and the other spirits are dead, in our world where we are now we are still alive. My name is Patrick, by the way.'

'It's nice to meet you Patrick' said White Angel, and she shook his hand. 'And it's a pleasure to meet you too' said the spirit.

'Right, I'd better go and finish rescuing those people down in the cave' said White Angel.

'Do you need any more help?' asked the spirit.

'No, Patrick, it's OK, but thank you for everything.'

'You know where we are' said the spirit. 'Just call if you need us.'

'I will.'

When she got back to the cave, she called out that everything was clear and safe now. 'Send the men and women up Gail.'

One by one the prisoners' feet started to lift and then they flew over the black steps and out of the black gate. As White Angel watched them going out of the gate, she could see the relief in their faces as they were leaving the cave. Finally the men and women were all out. Gail then came out of the cave and Magdalene was right behind her.

'Right everyone' said White Angel. 'I want you all to hold each other's hands while you're flying so that no one will float away. OK?' The men and women nodded their heads.

'Right then', said White Angel. 'Let's go.'

So they all held each other's hands and started flying. As they were approaching the water, the strangest thing happened. The water that had been so black suddenly turned a deep blue colour with shades of pink here and there. The darkness had disappeared.

'Listen everyone', said White Angel. 'We are going to land on the water. If anyone is afraid of the water, there's no need to be, because you won't go right into it.'

Finally everyone was standing on the water.

'Did you do that White Angel?' asked Gail.

'No, I didn't do anything' said White Angel. 'Do you know, it's always been foretold that this place is really alive, and maybe it's true. Maybe it just needed some magic again.'

'It's certainly a lot brighter' said Gail.

White Angel decided that the best thing for them to do was to stay for a night so that the men and women could rest. So she closed her eyes and concentrated, and then wished for a big house. When she opened her eyes, there was a huge white house next to the water.

'Right everyone' said White Angel. 'Let's go inside.'

They went in to find that everything they needed was there. The living room was huge, and it had a couple of blue sofas and a few blue chairs in it. The room was yellow and the carpet was a light blue colour, and there was also a television. The kitchen was a nice shade of green. There was a cooker, fridge, freezer, microwave and a kettle and plenty of food. There were eight bedrooms and they all seemed to be the same colour - lilac. Each room was carpeted and had three single beds in it.

Gail went into the kitchen to make everyone something to eat. The men and women they had rescued were so thin that they were like skeletons. You could see their bones pushing through the skin.

Gail called to White Angel and as she went through to the kitchen, she said: 'Something smells good Gail. What are we having?'

'Pasta with potatoes' said Gail. 'I reckon that that will fill them up.'

'It certainly will' said White Angel. 'Anyway, what did you want me for Gail?'

'Well I was just wondering. Do you think all of them will make it? Some of them look so ill.

'We will just have to wait and see. If God chooses to take them, he will. There is nothing we can do about it. We can only nurse them and try and help them.'

'But White Angel, wouldn't our powers help?' said Gail.

'There is a limit to what our powers can do. Although our powers are very strong, these men and women are really ill. And who knows how long they were down in that cave? It could have been years. It's sad to say, but because these people are so ill, our powers are not strong enough to help them.'

'But I helped my mum when she was in pain?'

'This is different Gail' said White Angel, a tear running down her face. 'These people have been ill for so long, that it would take a miracle to help most of them. They're all in God's hands now.' Gail looked at White Angel and said: 'I understand.'

The pasta and potatoes were ready, so Gail put most of the plates and cutlery on a big tray and put the food out on to it. Then she carried the tray into the living room and gave the men and women their food. They were sitting with quilts wrapped around them. One of the men thanked them, but it took all his energy to say it.

Gail's eyes were full of tears. She put her hand on his shoulder and said: 'You're welcome sir', and gave him a smile.

'Right', said White Angel. 'Let's go and give the others their meals. I just hope that they will have the strength to eat all of it.'

They then went upstairs and entered the first bedroom. A woman was lying in one of the beds, Magdalene sitting next to her. The woman's face was pale and she was fast asleep.

'Do you think we should wake her up to give her something to eat?' said Gail to her grandmother.

'No, Gail. We are better leaving her just now. Let her rest.'

The look on Magdalene's face was sad, as if she knew the woman wasn't going to make it. Magdalene stood up and said a prayer, and Gail and White Angel joined in. Then Gail and White Angel went into the other rooms and gave everybody their meals. Most of the men and women needed assistance, so Gail and White Angel sat down beside them and helped them with their food. Some of them managed to eat by themselves, though they were struggling really hard.

Later on that night when the men and women were sleeping, Gail made some more pasta and potatoes for herself and White Angel.

'What about you, Gran?' said Gail. 'Can you eat?'

'No, unfortunately I can't, but I know it would have been nice if I could have tasted it, because it smells good', said Magdalene.

White Angel closed her eyes and wished for a kitchen table and chairs. She opened her eyes to find a white table and chairs right in front of her.

'Now we can sit down and eat' said White Angel.

'Gran, can I ask you something?' said Gail.

'Yes Gail, what is it?' said Magdalene.

'How are you able to lift the kettle and the cups and other objects, as how you are a ghost now?'

'When you die and you cross over to the other world, you have new powers. It's strange and exciting. We can go anywhere we want and move anything we want. Like you and White Angel, I can move things with my mind. Does that answer your question?'

'Yes Gran, it does.'

It was very late and they felt shattered, so Gail and White Angel decided to get some sleep. They went into one of the rooms. Gail lay on top of one of the beds and White Angel on another and they fell asleep right away.

An hour later, Magdalene went up the stairs to check that Gail was getting some sleep. When she opened the bedroom door she saw that she was still in her clothes and was lying there with her arms folded. Magdalene used her powers by lifting Gail up, and as she was floating in the air, Magdalene lifted the covers and slowly moved Gail back under them.

'That's better' Magdalene thought to herself. She went over to White Angel and did the same thing for her. When she started to move White Angel with her mind, she saw white sparks coming from her.

'Wow', she said to herself quietly. 'That was incredible.'

Magdalene then went to check on the woman who had not been doing very well. She sat next to her bed and held her hand and told her not to be afraid. 'You'll be at peace very soon and your pain will be gone' she whispered to her. She knew this was the last night of the woman's life.

Then the bedroom door opened to reveal a woman standing there. She was an older woman with greyish hair and pale blue eyes. She was wearing a dark blue coat with a white blouse underneath and a dark blue skirt and black patent shoes. She went over and stood at the other side of the bed and looked at Magdalene.

'I'm Margaret, her mother' she said. 'I'm here to take her back with me.'

'Yes, I know' said Magdalene. 'Tell me something. What is her name?'

'It's Patricia' said Margaret.

'Being so ill, she couldn't even tell us her name', said Magdalene.

'I know. I want to say thank you so much for looking after her. I'm so glad that someone as kind as you was here for her. At least when she dies, it will be in peace.'

'I'm just sorry that we couldn't have done more for your daughter' said Magdalene.

'You've all done as much as you could' said Margaret. 'She will be joining me soon, and we can be together forever. I do hope the other people you rescued will be OK.'

'Yes, me too' said Magdalene.

Margaret kissed Patricia on the cheek and took her hand.

'Patricia, it's Mum. I'm here for you I'm going to take you back with me.'

Just then Patricia smiled, her eyes still closed. Then her spirit floated out of her body and she looked down at the shell she had left behind. She went over to her mother and kissed her on the cheek.

'I love you Mum' she said.

'I love you too Patricia' said Margaret.

Patricia went over to Magdalene and took her hand. 'Thank you Magdalene for taking care of me. I'll see you in the spirit world' she said.

'You will' said Magdalene.

Patricia floated towards her mother and took her hand. They started to fade away until eventually they were gone. Magdalene felt both sad and happy for them both.

She went to check on the others. They were all fast asleep, so she went down the stairs to the living room, finding the people there were asleep on the sofas. She went through to the kitchen and sat down at the table.

As she looked out of the window, she could see a blue and pink sky with stars. The sky seemed as still as a photograph. She then closed her eyes and thought about her past life on earth, and a tear slowly rolled down her cheek and fell on to her pale hand. She knew that her time was nearly up and that she would need to go back to the spirit world.

She heard movement from upstairs and knew it was Gail, so she put the kettle on for her and then put some lemon tea into a cup. Gail came down the stairs and went straight into the kitchen.

'Good morning Gran.'

'Morning Gail', said Magdalene. 'I've made you a nice cup of lemon tea.'

'That's my favourite Gran.'

'I know' said Magdalene. 'I've seen you drinking it when I came to
visit you back home. You couldn't see me, but sometimes I think you
could sense that someone was there. I could see it in your eyes.'

'You're right, I did think someone was there at times. Now
I know it was you, it makes me feel so happy that you were
there watching over me and Dylan. Thanks Gran.'

'You're welcome Gail.'

'Do you know something Gran? When I woke up this morning I was
looking for Dylan because he is usually by my side. When I realized I was in
a different room, I knew I wasn't at home and that Dylan wasn't here.'

'I'll tell you something Gail' said Magdalene. 'Dylan
is a stunning dog. He is definitely unique.'

'Yes he is Gran', said Gail.

'I would just like to say Gail that I'm so glad you and Dylan are
away from that horrible place. You are much happier now, and you
deserve to be. Your mum seems to be much happier as well.'

Someone called out from the living room, so Gail and Magdalene
went through to see them. A man was sitting up on the sofa.

'Hello sir' said Magdalene. 'Would you like a cup of tea?'

'Yes please' said the man quietly.

Magdalene went into the kitchen and made a pot of tea for
everyone. Gail sat down on the sofa next to the man.

'What's your name?' she said. 'Can you tell me?'

'It's Larry' said the man.

'It's nice to meet you Larry. My name is Gail and the other lady you saw
is Magdalene. Tell me something, do you remember how you got here?'

'Yes', said Larry. 'This man took me in my dreams and took me to
this place and tortured me. I can always remember when I woke up. I was

so relieved to be lying in my own bed in my own home. But one night he took me for real, and this time I did not wake up in my own bed. My body would have just disappeared, as if I had never even been there. I haven't seen my wife in a long time. Keeping her in my mind is what kept me alive. I couldn't believe that dreams could actually take you away.'

'Well maybe now you can go home Larry' said Gail. 'We will help you. OK?'

'You can help me?' said Larry.

'Yes, we can', said Gail.

Just then Magdalene came into the living room with tea and toast on a tray. She poured the tea into the cups and then gave the men their tea and a few slices of toast.

'I'm just going to go up the stairs to check on everybody and give them their tea and toast' she said.

'OK Gran', said Gail. 'Listen, since you're going up the stairs, could you check if White Angel is OK? She's been sleeping a long time.'

'It's the first thing I'll do' said Magdalene. She went up into the room where White Angel was and saw that she was still sleeping. Magdalene looked at the white clock on the bedroom wall and saw that the time was a quarter to ten. She left the room and closed the door. Then she went into all the other rooms to give the men and women their breakfast.

She couldn't believe the change in those people. They seemed so much better and didn't look so tired. The cuts on their faces had vanished.

After they had had their tea and toast, they went down the stairs to the living room. Gail was in the kitchen, making more tea.

'Is White Angel out of bed yet?' asked Gail.

'No, she's still fast asleep. I think we should give her another hour before we wake her up.'

'OK' said Gail.

After Gail had poured the tea into the cups, she gave everyone their tea. She then sat down on the sofa next to one of the younger women and said: 'Hi, I'm Gail. Can you tell me your name?'

'My name is Anna.'

'Well it's really nice to meet you Anna' said Gail.

'And it's nice to meet you too Gail' said Anna.

'How are you feeling?'

'A lot better than I was.'

'That's good to hear. I take it you got to know these other people quite well?'

'Well, we got left alone a lot and now and again we would try to talk to each other, but because we were in so much pain, it was hard' said Anna.

'I can understand that', said Gail. 'Well you're free now. Do you have any family?'

'No, it's just me', said Anna. 'My mother and father are dead. They've been dead a long time now. I wished all the time for God to take me when I was chained to the cold red walls so that I could be with my parents.'

'Well it's over now' said Gail. 'You will never suffer again. We'll get you back to where you belong, OK?'

'OK' said Anna with tears in her eyes.

Finally White Angel came down the stairs and yawned. 'What's time is it? I feel as though I've slept for a hundred years.'

'It's eleven o'clock' said Magdalene. 'Here is a cup of tea and some toast for you.'

'Thank you' said White Angel. 'One of you should have woken me.'

'We thought it would be best to let you sleep' said Magdalene.

'I can't believe how well those men and women look', said White Angel. 'Last night I had a strange dream. All the men and women were standing in a circle and in the middle of it I was standing next to this man who looked like a wizard. He was wearing a long white hooded cloak and had long white hair. He was holding a staff and one by one he pointed the staff towards each of the people. Suddenly a bright white glow went through all their bodies and a powerful wind seemed to come from nowhere and sparks were flying from all around us. It lasted for a good few minutes, and then I woke up. It felt real, as if it actually happened.'

'That's because it did happen', said Magdalene. 'God came to you in your dreams in the form of a wizard so that he could help you and those people too, and as you can see you both succeeded. Well done.'

'Thank you', said White Angel. 'I'm so glad the dream was real. I feel privileged that God came to help me. And I'm happy for those men and women.'

After the people had finished drinking their second cups of tea, White Angel said: 'Right everyone. Do you all feel well enough to go home?'

'Yes' they all said.

'OK, it's really quite simple' said White Angel. 'What you all have to do is take each other's hands and one by one you'll all vanish. Now don't be afraid. There's nothing to be frightened of, I promise. When you go back home, you will find that you will get better quickly. Try to eat plenty. I know it will be hard at first, but you all need to put on some weight. At least your cuts and bruises have gone and you aren't in any pain any more. Your body and your mind have healed quite well, but you will all need to put weight on fast.

'When you get back home, your families will obviously ask where you've been. You all know that if you tell them the truth, they won't believe you. You will all have to just say you went away for a while. It's a shame you can't tell them the truth, especially after what you all have been through.

'Now and again you will catch a glimpse of me in your dreams. That will be me watching over you.'

All of a sudden the men and women found themselves dressed in new clothes. 'How the hell did that happen?' said Anna.

'Well I'm a witch and I have special powers, so I thought I would give you all new clothes' said White Angel. 'After all, every one of you deserves a treat.'

They all thanked her. Then she said: 'OK everybody. Gather around. Gail, Magdalene, if you want to join in, you can, but just make sure you let your hands go when everyone starts to fade.'

They all stood in a circle in the living room and held hands.

'Now everyone, I want you all to tell me your names one by one.'

Anna said her name first and then a woman called Elizabeth called out her name. Then there was Lucy and next to her was Rose, then Sheila, then Linda, then Maureen and Sarah. Then came the men - Sam, Larry, John, David, Wayne, Robert, Scott, Stephen, Greg, Michael, Craig, Vincent, Peter, Victor, James, George, Jonathan, Christopher, Mark and Brian.

'Gail, Magdalene, say your goodbyes now.'

Gail and Magdalene said goodbye to all the men and women, and then all of a sudden everybody started to shake and there came a powerful wind. Sparks were flying from White Angel.

'Everyone close your eyes and try to concentrate except you, Gail and you Magdalene', said White Angel.

The men and women began to fade a little and White Angel called out: 'Gail, Magdalene let go of their hands now.'

So Gail and Magdalene let go, and White Angel called: 'Right everyone, hold hands tightly.'

The wind got stronger and one by one the people all began to disappear. When they were finally all gone, White Angel opened her eyes and the wind suddenly stopped. She sat down and said: 'I'll tell you something. Sending all those people back has taken it out of me. There was so much concentration.' Gail got her a drink of water and said: 'Here you are White Angel. Take a drink of this.'

'Thanks Gail' said White Angel.

'Do you think they'll all be OK?' said Gail.

'Yes, they'll be fine. At least they're back home now where they belong, and I know all of them are just grateful to be alive. And now the war is over. It's time for us to go home as well.'

'What about this house?' said Gail.

'When we leave here, it will just vanish' said White Angel. 'One thing though, now that the darkness of this place has been lifted, I think we should make use of it rather than just leaving it the way it is. It would be such a waste.'

The three of them left the house. 'Gran, are you coming back home with me?' asked Gail. 'Mum would love to see you.'

'Yes I think I will', said Magdalene.

'Right, it's time for me to go Gail' said White Angel. 'Take care of your gran, OK?'

'I will' said Gail.

White Angel gave them both a hug and then off she went flying into the blue and pink sky. She called out: 'I'll never be far away.'

'Right gran', said Gail. 'Let's go.'

They flew off into the sky in another direction. As they got higher, they could see a rainbow with stars all around it, which made it look really magical. Gail couldn't wait to see Dylan again and for her gran to meet him. They seemed so close to the stars that they could touch them.

'We are nearly there Gran', said Gail.

From a distance Gail could see the moon. It was so bright that you would have thought someone was up there shining a torch. When they reached it they flew downwards across the ocean.

'What a view!' said Magdalene.

'I know, it's incredible. There's Katie's cottage down there.'

They flew down and landed right outside it.

'Are you OK gran?' asked Gail.

'Yes, I'm fine Gail, said Magdalene. 'I'm just a little nervous about how your mum is going to react when she sees me.'

'She'll be so excited to see you Gran, believe me.'

Gail knocked on the door. 'Who is it?' called Ellen.

'Mum, it's me Gail.'

Ellen unlocked the door and opened it. 'Gail, it's so good to see you' she said, and gave her a hug.

'Mum, look who's beside me', said Gail.

Ellen turned her head slightly and her own mother.

'Mum? Is that you?'

'Yes, Ellen, it's me. I came back because I wanted to see you again.' Ellen gave her a big hug and said: 'I can't believe it. You're actually here.'

Inside the cottage, Dylan was going mad. He knew Gail was home. She took away the protective shield around the animals.

'Who's my boy?' said Gail. 'Come on Dylan.'

He went up to her with his tail wagging, jumping up and down. He was so excited to see her. She hugged him tightly and said: 'I've missed you Dylan', and he barked four times as if to say that he had missed her too. Then little Lucky went over to her and was purring and rubbing

up against Gail's leg. Gail let go of Dylan and lifted Lucky up and gave
her a hug as well. Then she went over and stroked the rabbit.

'I've got a name for you, as I promised' she said. 'I'm going to call you Misty.'

Gail then went into all of the rooms and removed the shields with
her mind. Down in the living room, everyone was sitting talking.

'How are you Katie?' asked Gail.

'I'm fine. It's so good to see you Gail.' She gave her a cuddle. 'Dylan pined
and pined for you. It took us a lot of effort to try and get him to eat his food.'

'Well I'm home now and glad' said Gail. 'I'm just going
to put the kettle on to make some tea for us.'

'Don't you bother Gail' said Katie. 'I'll make it. You take a seat and relax.'

'Doesn't Gran look great, Mum?' said Gail to Ellen.

'She certainly does.'

'I told your mum and Katie all about what happened with the
demons and the devil and those poor people' said Magdalene.

'It's such a shame Patricia died' said Ellen.

'I know, but at least Gran was with her', said Gail.

'It was the least I could do' said Magdalene. And guess what
happened, Gail. Her own mother came for her from the spirit
world, and she sat down at the left side of the bed holding her
hand. Then she took her back to the spirit world with her.'

'That sounds fascinating' said Gail. 'I just wish I had been in the room with
you. It would have been so special to see. I'm just so glad you were there with her.'

'Yes, me too' said Magdalene.

Katie came into the living room with the tray and put it on the
coffee table. 'There's a cup of lemon tea here for you Gail' she said.

'Great, I'm really thirsty', said Gail.

'Can I ask you something Mum?'

'Yes, what is it?'

'Do you see Dad?'

'Yes I do' said Magdalene.

'How is he?'

'He's fine. Sometimes he comes and visits you on his own, but most of the time we visit together. He misses giving you cuddles. You were always his favourite little girl.'

Ellen looked at her mum sadly and said: 'I miss him too. You know mum. It's a miracle you being here. I would like to thank you so much for helping Gail.'

'Well, she is my granddaughter. I would do anything for her' said Magdalene.

'I know you would' said Ellen.

'Are you going to be staying here for a while, Gran?' asked Gail.

'Maybe just for tonight Gail, because I've got to return to the spirit world. It's where I belong now.' Ellen's eyes were full of tears.

'Don't cry Ellen' said Magdalene. 'I'm never far away.'

'The next time you come and visit, could you show yourself again?' asked Ellen.

'Maybe I had to show myself this time to help Gail, but I do promise that when I come back to visit you, I will do my best to show myself to you, and if I can't I will make sure you know I'm there' said Magdalene.

'That would be good enough for me' said Ellen.

'So Gran, what do you think of Dylan?' asked Gail.

'He's a wonderful dog and so white. His ears are just like silk' said Magdalene.

Dylan was all over her. She gave him a cuddle and said: 'Aren't you a lovely boy?'

'Woof woof!' said Dylan, and he gave her a paw.

'You're very clever, aren't you Dylan?' said Magdalene.

'Woof woof' said Dylan again.

Everyone was absolutely shattered, and they all went to bed. That night Gail had a peaceful sleep, and there were no demons or devils in her dreams.

The morning soon came and Gail woke up. She looked at the clock beside her; nine thirty. Dylan was lying right beside her on the bed. She got up quietly, trying not to wake him, but as soon as she opened the bedroom door he woke up and jumped off the bed.

'Come on Dylan, let's go and get some breakfast.'

He barked as if to say OK.

'Quiet Dylan, you might wake everyone up' said Gail, but when she opened the kitchen door, Ellen and Magdalene were already sitting at the kitchen table.

'Morning Mum, morning Gran.'

'Morning Gail.'

'I didn't know anyone was up, it was so quiet.'

'We spoke quietly so we wouldn't wake you or Katie up' said Ellen. Gail put the kettle on and asked if her mum wanted more tea. 'No thanks Gail', said Ellen.

'I would have offered you tea Gran, but I know you can't drink it' said Gail.

'That's right Gail. Unfortunately I can't.'

Gail opened the back door to let Dylan out and said: 'Gran do you want to come and see the dolphin waterfall?'

'Yes, that would be nice', said Magdalene.

'It's over here, near the bench Gran.'

'It's really quite impressive, isn't it?' said Magdalene.

'Yes it is Gran', said Gail. 'Do you know, the dolphins that used to be in this waterfall were real. I thought to myself that they should be free, so I released them into the ocean and as you can see, I put ordinary dolphins there instead.'

'That was a special thing to do Gail' said Magdalene. Well, I've got to go now.'

'Oh, do you have to?'

'Yes, Gail, but as I said to your mum, I will come back and visit you.'

She hugged Gail and kissed her on the cheek and said 'I'd better go and say goodbye to your mum.' She went back inside. Ellen and Katie were both now in the kitchen.

'I need to go now Ellen', said Magdalene.

'I know Mum.'

Magdalene went over to Katie and gave her a hug. 'It was really nice to meet you Katie' she said. 'Take care of yourself.'

'You take care too' said Katie.

Magdalene then approached Ellen and gave her a hug and said: 'I love you Ellen, and I want you to know that I'll always be here somewhere watching over you.' Ellen started to cry.

'Please don't cry Ellen' said Magdalene, giving her a handkerchief.

'You could stay with us Mum, I know that you would love it here' said Ellen.

'If I could I would, but I have to go back to the spirit world, because that's where I belong now.'

Magdalene went over to Gail and gave her a hug. Then she bent down and gave Dylan a hug as well. Then she went over to Ellen.

'Remember I love you, and I won't be far away' she said. She began to fade.

'Tell Dad I love him' said Ellen.

'I will' said Magdalene.

'I love you Gran.'

'I love you too Gail.' Magdalene blew her daughter a kiss and was gone.

Gail held her mother. 'It's OK Mum. Gran will still be around. You'll feel her presence sooner than you think. Spirits which are close to us always stay near.'

'In a way, I felt as if I was letting her go again like when she was alive and was ready to cross over' said Ellen.

'I understand.'.

'Let's all go down to the shore and let Dylan and Blacky go for a swim' said Katie.

'Yeah, that sounds good' said Gail. 'What about you Mum, do you want to come?'

'OK Gail' said Ellen.

'Before we go though, I'm going to check on the dogs and cats and the wildlife.'

Gail put her hand across her face, and concentrated until she could see the dogs' house. She then removed the shield from around the house, and by using her mind, she went into the house. The dogs were fine. Some of them were sleeping and some were lying out in the back garden. There was plenty of food and water for them. When she had removed the shield from the back of the house, she went to the cats' house and went through the same procedure. The cats were fine as well, as were the wild creatures. She removed the rest of the transparent shields and the spells she had used to protect all the animals from fear. So now all the animal spells were broken.

Finally, when she was done, she said: 'Right, let's all go now.'

'I take it all the animals are OK?' said Katie.

'Yes, they're fine' said Gail.

Gail then lifted up Lucky and little Misty. With Dylan behind her, off they went. When they got to the ocean. Gail could hear the dolphins from a distance.

'I can't believe I nearly forgot' she said.

'Forgot what?' said Katie.

'I nearly forgot to remove the shield from the dolphins.'

She removed the see-through shield and the dolphins had the rest of the ocean to move around in again. She could hear them getting nearer to her. Then they suddenly came right out of the water. There were so many of them now. Gail took her sandals off and went into the water, and the dolphins came right up to her. Gail stroked them.

'Hi Precious, hi Lightning' she said. 'I see you've had more babies.'

She splashed around in the water with them for a good while. Dylan was swimming not far from where Gail was. He wasn't afraid of the water any more. The spell Gail had put on him so that he wouldn't be afraid of the water had worn off, but now he had lost his fear. She was so pleased that he was swimming on his own now, and that he wouldn't need her help any more.

Dylan followed her out of the water.

'I enjoyed that', said Gail. 'What about you Mum? Aren't you going in even for a paddle?'

'No, I don't feel like it Gail' said Ellen. 'Anyway I've been looking after Lucky and the rabbit.'

'I forgot to tell you Mum, I named the rabbit Misty.'

'That's nice.'

'Yes, I think so' said Gail. 'Where is Katie?'

'She went for a walk with Blacky' said Ellen. 'She said she wouldn't be long.'

'I can't wait to sleep in my own bed tonight Mum' said Gail. 'I just hope the scary dreams stay away, at least for a while.'

'Well now that the war is over, you should sleep peacefully', said Ellen.

'I hope so.'

'There's Katie now' said Ellen. Blacky was running towards Gail.

'Hi Blacky' she said. 'You're a lovely boy aren't you?'
She stroked him. 'Hi Katie. Are you feeling OK?'

'I'm fine' said Katie. 'Would you both like to come back to my cottage for some dinner?'

'That would be nice' said Ellen.

They sat for a while on the golden sand and watched as it glistened in the sun. It was soon five o'clock, and they all went back to Katie's cottage, where Gail helped her prepare the dinner. They made soya mince with potatoes, and as Gail was putting the food on the plates, Katie gave the animals their dinner. When their own meal was ready they sat down at the kitchen table and ate their dinner.

Afterwards when they had finished eating, they went through to the living room.

'I think we should all have a drink' Katie said. 'I reckon we deserve it.'

'We certainly do' said Gail.

So Katie went through to the kitchen and then came back into the living room with a bottle of Martini and three glasses. She poured out the Martini into the glasses and said: 'Here you are Gail.'

'Thanks Katie', said Gail.

'What about you Ellen?' said Katie. 'Would you like a Martini?' asked Katie.

'No thanks', said Ellen.

'But it's your favourite drink?'

'Yes, but I don't really feel like a drink.'

'Go on', said Katie. 'It's just the one drink to celebrate keeping our world safe.'

'OK then' said Ellen.

After a few drinks they were beginning to enjoy themselves. It was eleven o'clock when Gail and Ellen went home, Gail carrying Lucky and Misty. Back at the cottage, Gail suggested to her mother that she should sleep downstairs in case she hurt herself by falling down the stairs after having had a few drinks, and she agreed.

When Gail reached the cottage and opened the door, Dylan ran inside, excited to be home. Gail fed the animals and made herself a cup of lemon tea. When she had finished drinking it, she took Misty outside and put her in the hut, with her food and water beside her.

In her dreams that night Gail saw herself standing by the ocean, and on the surface of the water there was a cold mist. She could see a face in the mist. As it became clearer she saw that it was her gran.

Magdalene floated towards Gail and touched down on the sand, taking Gail's hands.

'I wanted to thank you for taking care of Ellen for me' said Magdalene.

'You're welcome, Gran' said Gail.

'I also want to say that I enjoyed my time with you. Who knows, maybe someday I will be able to come back again.'

'I hope you can Gran' said Gail. 'I really do. I want you to know that I really enjoyed you being here too. It's just a shame that you couldn't stay with us forever. You will always be in my thoughts, each and every day.'

Magdalene then went floating off into the mist. As she went through it, it began to disappear, and then Magdalene herself seemed to disappear with it. Then a brilliant star appeared in the sky. Gail looked up at it and smiled, thinking to herself that it was probably her gran watching over her. She closed her eyes and didn't dream for the rest of the night.

Meanwhile, back at Ellen's home, she was on the sofa sleeping when she suddenly woke up. She looked at the clock on the table beside her; three o'clock. She noticed a bright glow from outside the window, and then she could see a face. She wasn't sure who it was.

'Who's there?' she asked.

Just then the front door of the cottage opened by itself. Ellen got up from the sofa and hurried through to see who it was. A glow of the light went right past her and straight into the living room. For some reason, she didn't feel any fear. The face appeared, then the body. As the bright light disappeared, Ellen saw who it was.

'Dad, is that really you?'

'Yes Ellen, it's me.'

Her father was quite tall and was wearing a long brown raincoat and a brown hat. His shoes were also brown and very shiny. His blue eyes looked deeply into Ellen's.

'My child, I have missed you.'

'Am I dreaming?' said Ellen.

'No, you're not dreaming Ellen' said her father. 'I'm

standing here as real as you, but it won't last long.'

'Can I cuddle you dad?' asked Ellen.

He went up to her and put his arms around her.

'You were always my favourite Ellen, and your mum was right' said her father. 'We do come and visit you quite a lot. You just can't see us. When we show ourselves, it takes a lot out of us, which is why we don't show ourselves. But if you ever want me, just call. I'll be right here, but just not in body. Your mother and I don't want you to be sad for us. Just be happy that we are at peace now.'

'I am happy Dad' said Ellen. 'I really am.'

'I need to go now Ellen, but will you please tell Gail I said hello and that I love her, and I want all of you to know how proud I am that you kept this special world safe.'

'I will, Dad.'

'Well… goodbye Ellen.'

'Goodbye Dad.'

She stood there watching as the glow of light surrounded him and grew brighter until she couldn't see him any more. The light started moving slowly into the hall and then towards the front door. The door opened and the glow of light went outside and suddenly speeded up, moving rapidly up into the sky. Then it disappeared.

Ellen closed the door, tears falling from her eyes. She felt so privileged that her father had come to visit her. She then went back into the living room and went over to the window and looked up at the stars.

'Some magic is true. You've just got to believe, isn't that right Dad?'

Just then one of the stars began to change colour. Ellen knew in her heart that the star was a sign from her dad. She smiled and blew him a kiss.

'I hope one day I will see you again' she said. 'Who knows, maybe a little magic will bring you to me once again.'

the end

www.ingramcontent.com/pod-product-compliance
Lightning Source LLC
Chambersburg PA
CBHW070820250626

47170CB00006B/2172